Night to Dawn 48

I0521364

Marge Simon: pages 10, 41, 68, and 87
Chris Friend: pages 25, 53, 74, 85, and 90
Sandy DeLuca: front cover and pages 3, 17, 35, 70, and 89
Elizabeth Hattie Pierce-Collins: pages 31, 56, 76, and 94
April Lafleur: pages 21 and 60
Denny E. Marshall: back cover and pages 9, 37, 66, and 86
Vincent Davis: pages 30 and 88

Night to Dawn No. 48, October, 2025; Copyright 2025 by Barbara Custer. All rights revert to individual author and artist after publication. ISSN # 1542-1430; ISBN: 978-1-937769-90-1
Night to Dawn is a semi-annual publication of fiction, poetry, artwork, articles, and review.
Orders, editorial, and queries: Barbara Custer, P. O. Box 643, Abington, PA 19001
Email: barbaracuster@hotmail.com or ntdsubmissions@gmail.com
PayPal orders: venus1021@juno.com.
Submissions: ntdsubmissions@gmail.com; Web: www.bloodredshadow.com

Pickings and Tidbits

Top of the balloon to you! ☺

We went from a brutal winter to a blazing summer. However, walking outside in the heat, so long as I use common sense, won't send me to the doctor's office the way single-digit temperatures might. Moreover, vampires and other monsters become sluggish in the heat, and they are repelled by sunlight. I've been planting peppers and tomatoes and hope for a decent yield.

I'm looking forward to my favorite pumpkin treats in the fall, along with a chat with the Great Pumpkin. On to *Night to Dawn 48*, which includes SF tales as well as zombies and vampires.

A rhetorical question: does life exist in other worlds? Lee Clark Zumpe's "Truth" suggests this may be the case. I watched a documentary about the military sitting on files containing evidence of life from other worlds, which ties in nicely with "Truth." "Where Men Had Seldom Trod" reminds me that humans can be the worst monsters. I found the villains here scarier than vampires or even zombies, by far. This story is a serial, and the conclusion will appear in *Night to Dawn 49*. In Zumpe's story, "Infotosis," I think Mr. Quarta is a human vampire, a mighty one that our narrator wasn't prepared to encounter. Do human vampires exist in real life? I wonder. When one reads "The Forest of Katla," one may assume the fighters are trained humans; the narrator never mentions their species until the end, which delivers a powerful punch.

Night to Dawn tales often have a grim ending, but some of the stories have happy ones. The happiest ending for me is the reunion of long-lost lovers, and the ending in Charles Gramlich's "Soft They Were, and Broken" is especially poignant. Rod Marsden's "The Golden Hour" concluded with a dying man's kindness triumphing over hate. I loved Amari in Marge Simon's "Awaiting Them"—she was truly a Momma Tiger protecting her people. You might think twice about hiking through the woods after reading Linda Barrett's "Mike Walker," but the story ends on a flavorful note.

Margaret L. Carter's "Interview with a Reluctant Vampire" had a humorous aspect— when the victim drives away the vampire. Ditto for Matthew Wilson's "Diet or Die;" even monsters have their struggles with the waistline! I had to smile as I read Marc Shapiro's "Crime Scene Confidential." I couldn't help wondering if Detective Hardcase was a vampire; it takes one to know one.

Trigger warning: Harold Kempka's "Turkey Shoot" is suitable for the Thanksgiving holiday; however, one might not want to eat turkey after reading it. No happy endings here. Rajeev Bhargava's "We, the Possessed" is what happens when an earthquake's devastating consequences include cracks in the ground, opening the gateway to hell. This is part of a sequel that will continue through the following issues. I loved the twist ending in Marge Simon's "Eel Soup;" it sounds like the protagonist got more than he bargained for. Hillary Lyon's "In Widow's Weeds" had a grim ending, but not the way you might think. I suspect that the narrator is secretly grieving over the way her husband broke her heart. He sounds like a real scoundrel. Christopher T. Dabrowski's short "Small Differences" features science gone terribly wrong.

Sandy DeLuca contributed poetry and illustrated the front cover and interior pages. Denny E. Marshall did the back cover, interior illustrations, and poetry. Marge Simon contributed poetry, prose, and interior illustrations, while April Lafleur illustrated two of the stories.

Elizabeth Hattie Pierce continues to bring her incredible illustrations, and along with his own work, Chris Friend contributed some poetry. Vincent Davis is back with more of his comic strip illustrations, and I look forward to receiving more submissions from him. Kendall Evans is back, and I hope to see Kendall's work in the upcoming issues. Many thanks, balloons, and hugs go out to all the authors, poets, and illustrators who contributed to the magazine.

Good news department: Lyn McConchie's *One is One and All Alone* is being edited for publication, hopefully in the fall. *One is One* is an apocalyptic tale about a virus that decimates the human race. Michael De Stefano's *American Odyssey* has gone live and is available on Amazon and other major retailers. *American Odyssey* is a coming-of-age story about teenagers as they mature into adulthood. Along the way, there's lots of comedy and, alas, some tragedy.

"Night Gallery" features more movie reviews by Lee Clark Zumpe. I've promised myself one day to watch at least one of the movies. I hope you enjoy it.

I've avoided the shed since the last issue. It's been too cold to go outside unless I'm at the store chasing balloons. However, summer is here, and it's a good time to explore. My balloon-floating idea posed some problems—I had no way of steering myself to the house once I was up in the air. I think I'll go on foot, using my cane, which also doubles as a weapon. The shed is unlocked. Take my hand, and we shall explore the coming pages. ~ *Barbara Custer*

Truth
by
Lee Clark Zumpe

CONFIRMED: Life exists elsewhere in the universe
CONFIRMED: Natural selection has engendered the evolution of a race with intelligence which rivals our own

Thed's mouth dropped open.

He staggered, shuffling backward over the slick tiled floor a few feet. Dizzy and out of breath, he quivered uncontrollably, making the document tremble. He forced himself to read the words he had believed all along.

For so very long, he had waited for this moment. He had strived toward it, spending every bit of time and energy he could afford to reach it. The cost for this victory had been considerable. He had sacrificed so much.

An alarm awoke; its cry echoed through the corridors outside. Thed spun about, glancing at the door he had forcibly opened, and he realized he had spent too much time here. His utter amazement had jeopardized his mission.

Running along the long aisles of computerized files, he darted for the rear emergency exit which would take him away from the archives room. The aging mainframes clicked and spun and whirred as he raced by, their winking lights mocking him.

The words still whirled about his brain as he struggled to understand the consequences of this discovery.

HISTORY: Long range scanning devices detect signs of advanced technologies; evidence is obtained revealing unmanned probes are operating in and around the star system; two hundred forty-seven sightings, including twelve known instances of direct contact with the alien life form, are documented.
ALIEN DESCRIPTION: Witnesses report the aliens are similar to our own species, with the following exceptions: Skin tone is darker; eyes are smaller; the digits of the feet and hands have one less joint. Anatomically, the aliens share most of our physiological traits, though they do possess two additional organs the function of which has not been determined. A specimen is available for scrutiny upon request, level 018A6-A clearance required.

Thed had begun his quest for knowledge—for truth—while still in school. One of his instructors unwittingly ignited his passion by suggesting his interpretation of an "unexplained scientific phenomenon" paralleled that of a number of fringe theorists who "didn't know any better." It was the first time he had come face to face with the barrier of indisputable rationale: No matter what the line of logic he utilized, no matter how impassioned was his sermon, the instructor would not even admit to the possibility that his theory might be correct.

Another barrier threatened to stop him now: Faint red lasers crisscrossed a doorway which opened onto a rarely-used perimeter corridor. Though the lasers would not hurt him, they would set off additional alarms and trigger a shutdown sequence which would close off all passages in and out of the Records Office.

He shot a quick glance back and, finding no one following him, went to work on the control circuit. He had come well-prepared.

From a pack on his belt, he removed several small metallic instruments. The wall panel snapped from its place. His fingers played over multi-colored wires. He held cable snips in his mouth. With a few well-placed relays, and with the severing of the master control, the lasers in the door flickered and disappeared.

Thed didn't have much of a background in technology. His official education had taken another course. He had studied history, the languages, and literature. His primary scientific interest at the university had been astronomy.

It was with the Group that he had learned how to deactivate security systems. He also learned how to hack into high-level files, and how to obtain hard copies of those files without alerting the authorities. He learned about personal weapons. He was taught everything about the hidden military establishment, how it controlled the government. He learned about age-old conspiracies and coverups. He learned he had enemies.

Thed worked closely with the founders of the Group. He was influenced by their determination to make the truth known to the masses. Society, they had always believed, should be given access to all the information the government had buried. He believed that, too.

TECHNOLOGY: Reports have shown that the development of advanced technology by the alien race has paralleled that of our society. Since the procurement of several alien spacecraft, analysts have shown that much of their technology is comparable to that of our own; in some fields they have not made great strides, while in others they have excelled beyond our own capabilities.

A different alarm sounded. It was a biting, loud noise that made his ears hurt and his eyes water. He heard people shouting. The lockout system had failed. His sabotage had been successful. He smiled.

During the time he spent working with the Group, he met Ayria. By the time they were introduced, he had been promoted to the Board. The Board was comprised of the policy-makers and the teachers, and formed the leadership of the Group. During his tenure, he had worked with the other members of the Board to develop several schemes to force the government to exchange information the Group required to lend credence to their beliefs.

Ayria and he became intimate, even though the Group forbade their relationship. Sexual relations between Board appointees and lesser members of the Group had always been against policy.

Ayria died while carrying out one of his plots.

She and two other Group members were sent to capture a high-ranking government official. He was to be held hostage, and would be returned only if the information banks were opened wide for the public to study.

Ayria was shot during the kidnapping by a bodyguard.

He did not grieve for her. She had died doing what she believed in.

"Stop and drop!"

The voice startled him. He froze in his tracks. A single set of footsteps closed in on him from behind him. Moving slowly, cautiously. He could feel the blue laser dot on his neck, steady.

The soldier's boot tapped on the black floor.

Thed doubled over, his right hand grasping the pistol holstered on the inside of his left thigh.

A projectile sliced through the air above him; he heard a single *crack*.

His finger jerked.

His aim was keen.

The security guard's face split open; blood spattered the wall behind him. The body crumpled to the ground, shivering as if the air had grown intolerably cold.

Damn it! He thought to himself. His reaction had been too quick, too brutal. He might have talked his way out of the situation.

But was the gold in his hand worth the risk?

POLICY: It has been the unanimous decision of those in power to maintain a strict policy of non-interference. Observation and clinical study continue. From materials salvaged from the recovered spacecraft, we are augmenting our own technology. Military strategists are familiarizing themselves with the aliens' weapons systems and engaging in mock battles to determine the outcome of any invasion scenarios.

He ran on. He kept the weapon in hand.

Thed was not without regrets. It had been the abduction scheme that led to the destruction of the Group. The government's response to the kidnapping was to release a statement that the abductee had passed away of natural causes. The Group had miscalculated the value of this individual's life.

Looking back, their reaction seemed obvious. Thed and the Group were willing to give up their lives for truth — the government was clearly willing to make sacrifices for secrecy.

The Group made a second mistake. Since their initial plot failed, they released the abductee, hoping that his reappearance would show the treachery of the government.

He was plucked up by government agents before anyone could question his resurrection.

They must have gotten enough information out of him to lead them to the Group. One by one, members were apprehended. Some were re-educated; some were institutionalized; others just disappeared.

And, it is believed that once the officials had their information, the government abductee was put to death by his own government.

No loose ends.

Except one.

Somehow, they overlooked Thed. Their mistake would cost them.

He was pushing himself hard to clear the last possible security checkpoint. Once he was beyond that, he could filter out into the main arteries, mingle with the masses, conceal himself in hundreds of faces. He had obtained a single document that could unravel the elaborate tapestry of deception that had been crafted, a piece of paper that could bring people to their knees.

Where the Group had failed, a single man had succeeded.

Everything would be known. Eyewitnesses would come forward, no longer fearful that their testimony would result in threats of death or worse. The stories of the "fringe theorists" would be revisited, and with the new-found proof, would have to be reevaluated.

6

"There!" Someone shouted. There was a clattering of sorts, and a rush of activity. Uniformed soldiers poured out of an aperture not far in front of him. They knelt, brought up their weapons and took aim.

He did not bother to seek out cover. He would not have found any if he had taken the time. He felt his finger twitch, watched his weapon jerk in his hand. He heard the gun fire.

There were sparks and some smoke, and someone cursed. One of the soldiers reeled backward, dropping his rifle and clutching his side.

Something whistled by him to his right; he slowed, turned to look as it struck the wall behind him.

Something stung him in the neck.

The corridor became bright, and the walls fluttered. He felt his body fall out from beneath his head.

They gathered around him, the soldiers. Their commander stepped forward, snarling something at his troops. He grimaced into Thed's face, then began rummaging through his pockets.

No one noticed as he slipped a piece of paper and a computer disk out of Thed's possession and into a pack strapped to his side.

Thed bled slowly, silently.

He had failed ... but at least he knew.

Eventually, the secret would be revealed — the truth would be known. Others would learn about the conspiracy and the coverup, and they would learn about the Group.

The masses would someday know once and for all the truth about the supposedly "dead" planet their vast interstellar spaceship had been orbiting since its ageless journey to this solar system had reached its end. Perhaps they would even learn about his valiant attempt to put an end to the lies.

Someday, everyone would know: There is life on earth.

The End

The Other Pastime of Jack the Ripper by Lee Clark Zumpe

the name is inconsequential,
now: a century of bloodshed
muffles the screams of victims

and grainy photographs sprinkled
across collective memories
scarcely trigger a flinch;

but the Ripper found more than one
curious distraction, it must
be mentioned, in the shadowed

passageways off Whitechapel Road –
beyond the crowded markets
and freak shows, in darkened

doorways and gutters, set
at asymmetrical angles
and skewed unnaturally

against the quickening night;
in a labyrinth of deranged geometry
warping perception and sanity,

bending time and space...
with blood-slick fingers,
ancient formulae took form

upon grimy walls in hidden
alleys, opening doors to
distant shores where

the killer walked among
kindred souls, and madness
was not considered a weakness.

St. Andrew's Feast by Chris Friend

The priest
Drinks wine
With the thirst
Of a wolf fairy.
Outside the old Cathedral
The dead, dressed in puritan black,
Travel in great processions,
Leaving behind ossuaries
Empty as stillborn wombs.

Night Wanderer by Chris Friend

The Blue Fairy
Rides a coffin-shaped sleigh
Pulled by six black goats
That breathe gossamer steam,
And stop at each abandoned house
That stands solemn
As a tombstone
Marking where lost souls
Hide like bruised skin.

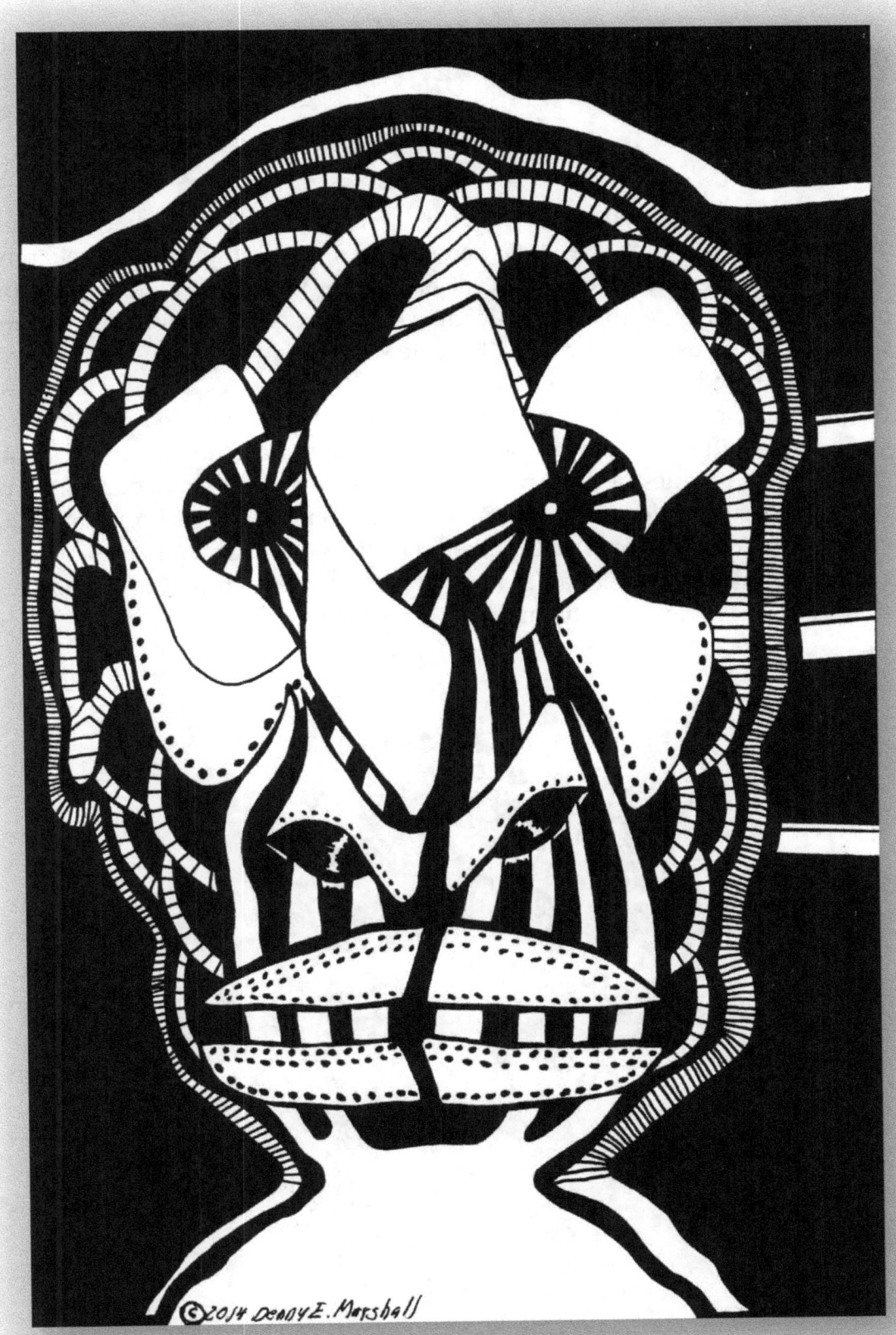

©2014 Denny E. Marshall

Awaiting Them
by
Marge Simon

Her name was Amari and she was worried. She alone perceived that another breed of vampires was moving through the stars, bent on subjugating humanity. Their power was mighty, for they were led by a descendent of Nosferatu. Why limit taking sustenance from mortals one at a time when, with careful breeding and strict containment, they might have an endless supply of precious life? Of course, his elite kind would not mix with the vampires of Earth, but were prepared to starve them to extinction.

This plan did not bode well for Amari's kindred. When she tried to warn them, they covered their ears. With no alternative, she made a certain magic in her orb of smoky glass, whispering words in tongues of the Ancient Ones. Earth became a confounding tapestry of shapes and signs with a single pulsing eye in the center. She led her kind through the eye to a new universe. When this was done, she blinked the old one out. Of course, the whole process of human evolution on the planet had to begin again at a freakish rate so they'd have sustenance. For Amari, that part was pretty much a piece of cake.

The End

Soft They Were, and Broken
by
Charles Gramlich

A black rain fell like nails from a burned-out heaven. It soaked the stony desert before fading. On the cold earth, a sheen of water turned to ice. At dusk, a man in scarred boots came crunching through the white frost. In his arms lay a body that silk had once loved.

When the moon had risen in a clearing sky, the man came to a Golgotha where the feathers of some gutted angel spread across the stones like snow. He set his burden down and straightened slowly, his back an aching knot of strained muscles.

Already, the one he sought had found him. He knew it from the singing that broke brittle in his ears. He knew it from the susurration of sand moving around him in the darkness.

"Come, demon," he called. "I've brought you an offering."

An acid-sweet chuckle stirred a breeze that pushed the man's long, dank hair back from his face. The breeze strengthened; shadows flapped like dark sheets; a whiff of honey and locusts swept past. His lips curled; he spat. Pushing back his blue jean jacket, he drew a snub-nosed Colt .38 from a nylon holster on his belt.

"Play no games with me, monster!" he snarled.

The chuckle became a laugh; the laugh became a woman formed out of fog and moonlight. Her snake-slanted pupils stabbed him like arrows. Her white limbs flashed in a boneless dance. Her body was nude and richly aroused.

"You cannot hurt me with such a weapon, human," the vampire said. Her voice came from everywhere and nowhere.

"But I can hurt me," he replied, lifting the pistol and placing the barrel to his temple. "The hollow point bullet in this gun is full of a bane that even your kind cannot swallow. I know you hunger. But if I pull this trigger, my blood will be spoiled for you. Unless … you agree to accept my offering."

The vampire hissed through pursed lips and flared nostrils. She drifted a few steps closer, then gazed down at the body laid out on the earth.

"This is no offering," she said, pointing at the corpse of a beautiful woman on the dirty stones. "I cannot take sustenance from one murdered in such innocence."

"I don't mean my wife," the man said. He lowered the gun. "I mean myself. Offered willingly. But in return, I demand a boon."

The vampire's eyes strobed red; she turned her head to one side, like a hawk studying some bit of prey that had surprised it by fighting back.

"What boon?"

He nodded toward his wife. "You raise her. Without giving her the hunger. I know you can do it."

"How do you know?"

He gestured at the feathers painting the desert. "It is said that you drank from an angel here. Found it dying, I imagine." He shrugged. "But you fed on it, stole its power. That's why you're chained to this place. And why you so desperately need what I'm willing to give."

"Blood," the vampire whispered.

"And freedom."

The vampire smirked. "And so much, much more. What is your name, human?"

"Blake," the man said.

"And I am Velaseia."

The man named Blake shook his head. "I don't care."

"You will," Velaseia said.

She floated toward him with a smile, showing jagged teeth in the porcelain face of a courtesan. Her luminous green eyes were marbled with black veins. Her scent overwhelmed him—dust and cacti, cinnamon and honeyed rot. She touched his arm, rousing a shudder. She leaned close and murmured a soft litany of obscenities against his ear.

He pushed the gun against his own ribs and put his finger on the trigger. "My wife first," he said. "*And* your promise."

The woman-thing drew away with a snarl. She spun toward the body of Blake's wife, her long black flag of hair flying. Kneeling, she leaned over the still form, examining it intimately. After a long moment, she looked up.

"It can be done. I can raise her without the hunger."

"Then do it."

Velaseia's body shivered. A glow pulsed through her skin like the beat of a molten heart. It brightened, delineating bones and organs within, not all of which were human. Buried in the flesh of the vampire's back, Blake glimpsed wings, folded and wrinkled, like those of a butterfly nymph inside a chrysalis.

Shocks tingled Blake's body. Dust lifted into the still air, winking like glitter under the moon. The vampire kissed Blake's wife on the mouth. A sound came next out of the silence — a single breath. Then another. A once-dead chest rose and fell.

Velaseia turned her head toward Blake, her face a ghastly shadow. Through a stain of fresh tears, the man saw the creature transform. Emerald eyes stormed; lips reddened and plumped like grapes; pale skin grew silver lines that writhed like animated tattoos. On spined feet, Velaseia rose. Smoke-black wings erupted out of her back. They beat the air in whispers.

Blake tossed his gun aside. He opened his arms; Velaseia swept into them. She pushed him back and down on the ground. Long-nailed hands ripped away his shirt and tore open his jeans. She straddled his waist. Lips that dripped venom lunged for his jugular. He caught the vampire's throat with both hands, held her at bay.

"Your promise," he said, his voice gruff.

The green eyes softened. "I promise."

Blake dropped his hands. He closed his eyes. Velaseia hesitated a moment. Then her hair entwined him like tentacles. She lowered her lips to his neck. Fangs gently dented his skin. A sharp tongue flicked like a snake's over the pulsing beat of his carotid.

"Do it!" Blake muttered through gritted teeth.

The vampire bit down. Blake snarled in pain and anger. But his hands grabbed Velaseia's hips, pulled her tight against him. Her body turned to smoke, solidified again an instant later with his sex buried in hers.

Velaseia's flesh was colder than frost. Then it warmed. It warmed. Blake cried out. Velaseia's fingernails stroked up and down his body, scraping gouges that filled with red. Her wings battered the air; her lips nursed at his neck while her hips pumped and thrust.

Blake opened his eyes. He growled, then shoved Velaseia away from his throat. Before she could respond in rage, he turned his head and took her mouth with his. His tongue pushed between her lips. The kiss that followed was full of want.

After a long, hungry moment, Velaseia drew back. "So you are willing," she murmured.

"I have to be."

The vampire nodded. She pressed her mouth to his again, and when his tongue came seeking, she parted her lips and took it. She bit down. Blood spurted. The taste and scent of copper and rust filled his senses. Every nerve and tendon surged with electricity. Blake's body arched up from the ground, caught for an immeasurable moment between ecstasy and agony.

Ecstasy won.

When all his muscles went loose, Blake closed his eyes. Velaseia had released his tongue. His head fell back and a smile smeared with blood curved his lips. His wife would live; he would die. That was all he cared about.

But he didn't die.

After a moment, Blake opened his eyes. Velaseia stood over him, her skin flushed with rose, her belly distended with blood. Her eyes flickered with some inner lightning; her wings slowly stroked the air. Blake frowned.

"Why am I alive?" he murmured weakly.

The vampire chuckled. "Did you really think you could bargain with me?"

Fear doused Blake. He tried to sit up but had no strength. "You promised," he tried to shout. It came out in a whisper.

Velaseia gestured, and Blake turned his head to see his wife rising from her bed of dirt. The white gown he'd dressed her in after her death gleamed like snow. Her hair sheened past her shoulders in a golden cascade. She was incredibly, wonderfully alive, but a look of confusion marred her beautiful face. She clearly didn't know where she was or how she'd gotten here.

Blake looked back at Velaseia, desperation coiling in his eyes. "Don't," he pleaded.

"I keep my promises," Velaseia said. "I won't touch her." She leaned down over the man, grasped his chin, and forced her gaze into his like the thrust of a saber. "But already you're turning. Your hunger grows." She laughed. "I won't touch her. You will!"

She released Blake's chin and pushed his head back against the ground. Her wings spread. She turned. In the next instant, she was gone like a streak of black light. Blake was alone with his wife. And his thirst.

Riley! Blake thought.

He wanted to call his wife's name out loud; he dared not. Then she saw him on the ground. She walked slowly toward him, seemingly confused as to who or what he was, but moving in her old, graceful way—alive, so alive.

Blake pushed himself to his knees and staggered upright from there. His legs offered little support at first, but strength poured steadily back into his body — an unholy strength. The change was sweeping through him, mutating every cell. He was becoming a vampire.

Riley paused as Blake rose. When she recognized him, a smile took her face. She started quickly toward him. He waved her back with one heavy hand. She kept coming.

"Stop," he called out, his voice breaking. Then, stronger, "Stop!"

Riley froze. Her smile fell into a concerned frown. "What is it, Blake? What's wrong?"

"Don't. Don't come any closer. I'm … I'm sick. You need to get away from me." Riley gasped in concern, took two fast steps toward him, then froze again as his voice boomed: "No!"

She held out her hands. "Let me help you."

"You can help me by leaving," he said, hating words that he deliberately made harsh, hating more the snarling undertones that had begun to invade his voice.

Hurt crossed Riley's features, but she shook her head. "You can't mean that. I won't leave you." She tried a small smile. "I don't even know where I am."

"In the desert. Outside of Phoenix. If you go north, you'll find the highway. But don't go back to the city."

Riley gasped again, louder. "Oh my God! The battle. I remember. Was it really … angels? Angels fighting angels?"

"Yes. Insane as that sounds."

"The end times!"

Blake shook his head. "I don't know. Maybe not. Right after the battle we saw, I heard a voice. A beautiful voice. It … told me things."

Riley's face took on a lost look. She glanced down. "I don't remember the battle ending. Or the voice. Why can't I remember?" Her gaze found Blake again. "How did I get here … how did we get here?"

Tears started in Blake's eyes, then dissipated. He was losing even that tie to humanity. Instead, his fists clenched. Fingernails daggered his palms. A spasm struck him, stole the words he wanted to speak. A red caul formed over his vision; the night grew dense with texture. Smell, taste, touch, sound, sight — intensified. Other senses, too, the likes of which he'd never dreamed.

To Blake's gaze, Riley glowed with eldritch light. He could taste her scent — of sweat, wounds, and innocence. He watched her heart beat through her nearly translucent skin. It throbbed with life, with crimson blood. In horror, Blake spat away the saliva filling his mouth.

"You have to go now, Riley. I'm sorry. But you have to leave me. If you don't, I'll … hurt you."

She shook her head. "No, you won't."

"You don't understand. I didn't want to tell you. But I have to. To make you understand. My God, Riley, you were dead! Killed in that awful battle! Stabbed through with some kind of spear. I pulled it out; I brought you here; I made a bargain. Your life for mine. If you stay, it'll be for nothing."

Stricken by her husband's words, Riley clasped her arms over her chest. A hundred emotions flashed across her face like frames from a movie. Twice she opened her mouth as if to speak, but no words followed. When she did say something, after a glacial moment of silence, it was no denial of his story. She only asked: "A bargain? With who?"

"A demon. A vampire! After the battle, the voice I heard. It told me. The vampire drank here from a fallen angel." He gestured to the angel feathers spread on the ground, only to find them gone, as if blown away by some invisible wind. It didn't matter. He continued, "The vampire was trapped here by the power it absorbed. I freed it with my blood. In return for raising you."

Riley trembled. Her lips vented a low moan. "Raising me? Raising me! As a vampire?"

"No!" Blake shook his head vigorously. "God, no! She brought you back without the hunger. Through the angel's power. That's what she gave you. You can live. Survive! But you have to get away from me."

Riley glanced down at her own body as if she'd never seen it before. She lifted her hands to study them, turning them this way and that. Blake recognized the moment when she began to believe. Her face creased in a frown, then smoothed. She met her husband's gaze, took a deep breath, and nodded as if to herself.

"It's okay," she said.

"No, it's not."

"Do you love me?" she asked.

"You know I do."

"Then trust me."

"Trust you in what?"

She held out her arms to him. "That you won't hurt me."

"No!" he protested, shaking his head. "I trust you, but I don't trust me." He held up his own hands for her to see. His fingernails lengthened into claws, then blunted back, then lengthened again. "I can't trust who I am now," he said. "Who I'm becoming!"

Riley took a quick step forward, caught Blake's hand before he could react. She drew it to her mouth, kissed the palm and then the fingers one by one. After a moment of shocked immobility, he tried to jerk his hand back, but her strength was suddenly immense.

She pulled their bodies closer, let go of her husband's hand but threw her arms around his shoulders. He grabbed her wrists and tried to break her hold. But she pressed her mouth firmly against his; her lips were tender and heated.

A surge of vicious hunger swept through Blake. His fingernails curved into talons around Riley's wrists. His lips were forced open as his incisors lengthened. He broke the kiss with his wife then, but stopped trying to push her away. He needed her close for what was to follow.

Blake's pupils must have been dilated as widely as caverns, for Riley shone in his vision like a bar of polished silver. Her eyes were closed, her head lifted, her lips parted. He could see the pulse beating beneath her chin. Again, saliva burst ripe in his mouth; this time he didn't spit it out. His teeth tingled with venom. He leaned toward her, to feed. Somewhere inside, a last human part of him was happy his wife's eyes were closed.

Riley reached down and touched the shaft of his penis. Her fingers wrapped around it and began a slow stroking. Blake stood there and shook, his teeth a bare inch from his wife's throat. He could feel the heat of her skin, of the blood beneath. He could taste it in the sweat that lifted like smoke from her pores.

"Love me," Riley whispered.

She stepped away from him. Her eyes were open now, gleaming like emerald mirrors. She lay down on the sand, her bare feet flat on the ground, her knees lifted. She held out her hands.

Slowly, as if in a daze, Blake kicked off his scarred boots and stripped away his jacket and the ruins of his jeans. He knelt at Riley's feet and rested his hands on her knees. His fingers tightened in the satin of her gown, bunching the material and pushing it slowly up her legs until it fell away to reveal her sex.

A blonde fluff of hair. A birthmark on the inner thigh, like a tiny red maple key. Memories surged in Blake's head. A wildflower meadow. Horses cropping grass. Lying with Riley in the dappled shade, his hands all over her, hers all over him. A dark creek under the moonlight. A deep pool where two naked lovers splash and kiss. A bedroom after a wedding. The slippery dampness of skin on skin. Scents of sweat and sex.

The needle teeth in Blake's mouth shrank back into the gums. A different kind of hunger swept him. He leaned down between Riley's legs and gently kissed the petals of her sex. His tongue flicked; Riley moaned. Her hands found their way into his long hair and tangled. His tongue flicked again, then faster. His mouth worked.

Riley arched her hips, crying out as she came. And while her back was arched, while her sex was liquid with pleasure and need, Blake slid up her body and stroked his shaft into her. She cried out again. Her eyes flung wide; her arms leashed around him, locking him to her.

"Fuck me!" she said.

Blake growled, but there was nothing animal in it, nothing more savage than the human need for joining. He thrust into her, deeply, fully. Her body met his. They found their personal rhythm and rode it together.

Then a new note entered. The friction of their skins whispered away. They moved together like fluid creatures, like waterborne spirits. And in the moment when all their empty spaces were filled, they sighed into each other's mouths and came.

From a distance, Velaseia watched the two lovers rise from their wild bed and walk hand in hand toward the north. Glancing into the sky, she turned her head as if hearing a distant voice speaking. She nodded agreement to whatever was said.

Her smoke-dark wings spread. She breathed. A sudden wind swirled around her, full of silvery feathers. When the wind passed, the vampire's wings were no longer black.

Wearing a wistful smile, Velaseia claimed a last glimpse of Blake and Riley walking toward their destiny. The couple's world had changed, but after tonight, they had the powers inside of them to shape it for the better — as was ordained.

With her wistfulness turning to joy, Velaseia soared into the moonlight.

The End

The Sleeping Princess by Matthew Wilson

Destroying Bathory's castle
One undisturbed coffin left
Marked DO NOT OPEN

16

Mike Walker and the Old Tree
by
Linda Barrett

One brisk, cold day, Mike Walker walked out of his apartment and through the parking lot. The surrounding forest was silent as he entered it. No birds sang. The only sounds were his footsteps crunching on the trail's gravel path.

Something eerie enveloped him. A chill of fear ran through him. Mike stood stock-still. An enormous tree blocked his path. The eerie feeling came to him from the tree. Its black bark made a cruel face at him. Another icy chill ran down his spine, and his heart pounded with fear.

Turning around, he ran back to his apartment. He slammed the door behind him and pressed himself against it.

"There's something evil in this forest!" he said loudly.

Later that day, Mike obsessed about the demonic tree. He mechanically swallowed his microwaved dinner. Each time he lifted his fork and opened his mouth, the tree haunted him.

He sat in an armchair in the lobby and watched tenants walk past him. They all wore face masks. He heard violent coughing all around him. He didn't want to become accustomed to it. Living with these old people made him feel sorry for them. For weeks, they suffered with Covid, and he prayed for them. When he told them this, they laughed.

"Mike, you're crazy!" one of the old ladies said. "It's just Covid."

"People die of Covid," he replied. "There's something strange about that forest. It's the big, black tree close to the apartment house. It's possessed."

Someone said, "There's no such things like demonic possession. Go home and take your medicine."

Mike went to sleep after taking his anti-psychotic medication. As he drifted off to sleep, a vision came to him. A burly Native American man planted a seed in what would become the tree. He pulled out a bag and sprinkled some dust on it. He chanted in his tribe's tongue and waved a wand over the plant. The big black tree went from a sapling to a giant tree within seconds. The Native American left and went back to his village. Mike realized the Indian was into black magic. The people in the village told him to leave. The chief in his war bonnet declared the gnarled-faced magician an outcast. The magician ranted and raved, then turned on his heels and left. Mike opened his eyes and sat up in bed. All he could do was gasp.

Mike's heart pounded as he crawled out of bed. He walked with wobbly legs to his bureau. He picked up his Bible and looked through the pages.

His eyes fell upon a passage from Isaiah 54:

"No weapon that is formed against thee shall prosper and every tongue that shall rise against thee in judgement thou shalt condemn. This is the heritage of the servants of the Lord, and their righteousness is of me, sayeth the Lord."

He sat in his favorite armchair at a corner of his bedroom and shut his eyes.

"Tell me what I should do," he breathed to Jesus.

Within the darkness of his closed eyes, he witnessed a group of young women wearing black robes surrounding the tree. They chanted about Satan and called him Lord. The tree grew bigger and bigger. Mike watched as two men dueled with pistols until one of them died on the spot. A young woman broke out in tears and fainted before the winner. He grabbed her by the arm and dragged her to a carriage. She dug her heels into the ground as he pulled her. Her beau lay dying. Mike went through the 19th century to the 20th, where a tableau of horrible occurrences took place under this tree. He couldn't make them out, but they were ugly. Workmen tearing down the forest faced horrible accidents as they built his apartment house. They left the big black tree standing. Mike noticed they were also afraid of it.

"What can I do?" Mike asked Jesus.

Mike waited patiently for the Lord's response. He waited until dawn. He heard only silence.

He put on his coat and squinted into the sunshine. Making his way toward the forest, he saw an ambulance rolling up to the apartment's driveway. The EMTs went into the building's front entrance. Mike watched them take out an old man in a stretcher. He hurried closer to see who it was. The old man wore a breathing mask over his mouth.

"Donald!" he shouted.

Donald looked up at Mike.

"Are you okay?" he asked Donald.

"They're taking me to the hospital. I got Covid." Donald wheezed. "I'm the sixth person on the third floor who has it. I'm asymptomatic. Please pray for me."

"That's enough, buddy," one of the EMTs said to Mike. "He needs to go to the hospital." They hoisted him into the ambulance and closed the doors after him. Mike's mouth dropped open, and his eyes teared up.

"He was like the grandfather I never had. This means war."

Enraged, Mike stormed up to the tree and punched its trunk repeatedly.

"How dare you kill that sweet, old man!" he shouted.

Mike looked down at his fists. Blood seeped from his knuckles. The tree seemed to laugh from deep within its trunk. Mike jumped back. His heart pounded with fear.

A verse popped into his head: *"Perfect love casts out fear."*

Falling to his knees, he prayed to Jesus.

"What can I do?" he asked the Lord.

Suddenly, he remembered that the local church's priest held Holy Communion for the apartment's residents every Wednesday at 11:30 a.m. His Timex watch let him know it was starting soon. He sped as fast as he could toward the church. The situation reminded him of Philip preaching to the Ethiopian eunuch in the book of Acts. He hoped the Holy Spirit would be with him.

Mike burst through the door and up the stairs to the social hall. The service hadn't begun, but everything was prepared. The priest went into the men's room. Mike picked up the chalice full of Communion wine and nearly knocked over an elderly resident as he fled out the door toward the forest.

A patrol car sped up to the apartment complex's driveway as Mike poured the Communion wine on the tree's roots. The two police officers grabbed him and pulled him back from the tree.

The huge tree emitted a low groan that caused the ground beneath it to rumble. Mike and the two cops fell onto the grass. They all watched as a massive fissure ran down the tree's bark. Molten blood spilled out and the tree screamed until it withered away.

"What's going on?" the priest shouted as he ran across the parking lot.

Mike sat up, laughing. "I'm sorry about everything. I just cast out a demon from a tree!"

"I can't believe this," one of the policemen mumbled.

"Neither can I. How did that tree die like that?" asked the other officer.

"That was strange," the priest said.

"Look!" Mike shouted, pointing at the smoking trunk.

A white lily rose from the fissure and perfumed the frigid winter air.

The priest looked down at the Communion cup.

"It's a miracle!" he shouted. "That's one heck of a vintage they gave me at St. Matthews! I should ask them where they got it from."

The End

The Escaped Demon by Matthew Wilson

I can't tell Mom about the demon
The monster beneath my bed
I didn't mean to free the thing
Now it's eaten the milkman's head.

I got the ugly book for Christmas
I read the words on page ninety-three
There came a hum and beam of light
And now the wicked thing is free.

Mother told me not to be naughty
When she left me in the house alone
So I will not tell her about the monster
The thing that bleached the gasman's bone.

There will be no Christmas if she notices
If she hears the neighbor's screams
So like all good boys, I go to bed early
And hope there'll be no ghastly dreams.

Turkey Shoot
by
Hal Kempka

The parking lot was empty when Bart left his client's office. Getting the proper order for the department store's holiday posters meant a hefty check, as they did not blink an eye when he gave them the price.

He and Carrie were leaving for the Thanksgiving holiday at his folks' house when he got home, and their bags were packed. He pulled into the driveway, and Carrie hurried from the house with an armload of luggage. He loaded the bags into the back and shivered in the icy wind of late fall.

The weather had made a sudden shift into winter mode, and a light snow flurry had begun. The dry chill hinted at the probability of a long and bitter winter. In addition, the holiday rush to get out of town meant traffic was going to be a bitch.

Carrie returned with a few other items while he threw their suitcases into the Land Rover's trunk. Bart had left it running, and when they jumped into the front seat, their faces flushed in the sudden warmth. After two hours of navigating through the slow-moving holiday rush on I-494, traffic thinned out. A few two-lane highways later, they drove across the black earth farmland of the southern Minnesota prairie.

Although the forecast had called for snow flurries, the gray day darkened, and a snowstorm hit without warning. Snow drifts began to clog the highway, and Bart plowed through, wrestling with the steering wheel while peering into the sudden, swirling near whiteout.

Their drive spiraled from joy and anticipation into a nightmare, as what should have been a two-hour trek to visit his family for Thanksgiving might now become four-plus hours. The bitter north wind defied the thick stand of barren oaks and cottonwoods that lined the highway as a windbreak for the tilled, barren cornfields. Sporadic gusts buffeted the car, and Bart's arms were tiring from fighting to keep the car on the road.

Up ahead, the first vehicles the couple had seen in twenty miles clogged the ditches along both sides of the road. Bart slowed the car to a crawl as they approached three abandoned vehicles and a jack-knifed big rig. Its nearly twisted-off cab jammed into the drifting, gritty snow like an ostrich with its head buried into the arid ground of an Aussie outback.

"Dammit! Black ice," Bart called out as the car began a slow swerving skid toward the passenger side.

He removed his foot from the accelerator. Carrie shuddered as the car drifted across the icy patches until again catching dry asphalt. While he straightened the car back into the lane, Carrie craned her neck to scan the accident scene. Blood stains marred the doors and windshields, and several windows were shattered.

"My God, this looks like something out of a horror movie," she said, grabbing Bart's arm. "Did you see all the blood?"

Bart shifted his gaze from the road to the cars and back to the road. "Yeah, I guess we'll have to be extra careful."

Bart accelerated on the dry pavement, and the tires hummed loudly against the asphalt.

Carrie looked back at the gory scene. "What's eerie is that we didn't see any people."

A wind gust swept a cloud of swirling snow across the road, and he nodded, keeping his gaze fixed on the road ahead.

"The state police must have transported them to hospitals and hotels."

She flinched and yelled, "Bart, look out!"

Carrie pushed against the seatback as two huge wild turkeys flew across the road and over the hood directly in front of them. Their high-pitched gobbles were loud enough to be heard inside the car, and their awkwardly flapping wings momentarily blocked the couple's view through the windshield. Although the slower of the two barely avoided hitting the windshield, it hit the sideview mirror with a loud thud, scattering a handful of tail feathers as the car sped past.

Carrie stared at the birds through the window and thought it odd how the clipped bird appeared to flash an angry glance back at the car before following the other one into the tree line.

"Whoa! Did you see the size of those birds?" Bart said. "If I had my shotgun, we would be bagging a fresh turkey to take to the family, just like in the pioneer days."

"Yeah, right, Bart," Carrie shot back. "Some pioneers we are. We're driving a Land Rover, and our idea of roughing it is checking into a lousy three-star hotel and buying lunch at a drive-through."

As dusk set in, the silvery frozen landscape turned somber gray. The barren trees cast ominous shadows across the road. Bart let up on the gas, letting the car slowly round a long curve.

They slowly drove past a car that had sheared off a road sign and spun into a ditch. A deep, jagged crease from the impact sliced through the front bumper and grill. The wooden sign pole had speared the windshield, and substantial blood patches soaked the snow.

Carrie noticed the side windows, which appeared to be riddled with holes, as though someone had shot them out.

"Oh, honey, look at that!" she said, her voice cracking. "I'm not kidding; this is getting scary. Maybe we should turn around and go back home."

"Nah, we've got four-wheel drive. If we take it slow and easy, we'll be fine. Probably some hunters were shooting at a pheasant, and errant pellets hit the car."

"You think we should call your family? They might be getting worried."

Bart handed Carrie his cell phone. "Yeah, maybe we should. Tell them we will arrive late tonight because of the storm."

She punched the numbers, but the "call failed" light kept appearing on the phone screen.

"Great, no signal," Carrie said.

They continued, with Bart watching the road while Carrie kept trying to get a signal. A muffled gunshot that sounded as though it was nearby broke the silence. In the waning light, another turkey flew across the road and disappeared into a stand of trees a little farther ahead.

"There must still be a couple of hunters out," Bart said. "I hope they don't mistake us for a turkey."

"That's not funny, sweetheart," Carrie replied.

She had no more than finished the sentence when several more shots rang out. Pellets peppered the Land Rover and shattered a back window.

"Son of a bitch! Hang on!" Bart hollered.

He accelerated but hit a patch of black ice. Bart eased up on the accelerator, but the Land Rover swerved to the right and began to spin. He steered into the spin, trying to regain control of the car, but it continued sliding toward the road shoulder.

A third shot punched a huge hole in the driver's side windshield. The top of Bart's head exploded like a melon, and Carrie screamed in horror. Gray matter and blood splattered her face as well as the headliner and back seat. He slumped forward on the steering wheel with bubbles gurgling from his mouth.

The car broadsided a road sign, and the passenger side door imploded on impact. Carrie screamed and shielded her face with her arms. The force slammed her into the crunching metal and glass shards, knocking her unconscious.

Carrie awoke lying outside the car in the snow. She choked on the blood filling her mouth and gagged. She tried to roll over but could not feel her arms and legs. Her lower body seemed paralyzed.

Warm, sticky blood trickled into her eyes, blurring her vision. She realized she could not have been unconscious for long and could make out the frozen surroundings in the rapidly waning twilight.

The air smelled curiously of blood and wet feathers. Carrie sensed someone standing over her and blinked her eyelids, trying to clear away the sticky, coagulating blood. Carrie's blood-curdling scream echoed through the frigid air as a grotesque-looking, costumed man stood over her.

A large patch of wrinkled skin hung below the chin from his leathery red face like a waddle. Rows of patterned brownish-black and white feathers hung from stocky, angled arms that cradled a shotgun.

Another, similarly dressed individual approached, jerking his head back and forth and canting it to one side. His dark, rapidly blinking eyes stared down at her. A knobby, pale pink waddle shook beneath a fleshy mouth that slowly curled into a sinister smile.

"I think we've bagged our limit, don't you think?" The massive birdman's gravelly and almost human voice echoed through a gobble.

"Yeah, put the filthy human out of her misery, and let's drag them back with the others. We have enough meat now to feed the entire flock," the other shadowy, hideous-looking creature replied in the same pseudo-gobble.

Another shot rang out and echoed through the trees. The hunters' turkey-like struts jerked at the corpses as they were dragged off into the night, leaving a trail of blood-stained snow. A chorus of gobble-like cheers greeted the hunters' return, and a couple of younger ones' argumentative voices rose above the din, debating over who would get a leg.

The End

Infotosis
by
Lee Clark Zumpe

The walls breathe. The air stifles. Florescent lights vie for surface space to illuminate. The sterile white tiles that carpet the floor quiver. Colors mingle and copulate; I pulse in the midst of it all.

I am positioned inside a support beam in the center of a spacious chamber. I am unseen by the uprights called *humans*. They could see me if they wanted to. It is only because they do not try to gaze beyond their experience and scan those depths just outside of their present comprehension that I am imperceptible to them.

It is best that I go unnoticed. I enjoy solitude and, revel in isolation. There is a certain degree of pleasure derived from being painfully obvious yet invisible. I am the ultimate impartial observer of this particular species. My colleagues admit I better understand their customs and social structure. I have knowledge of the most intricate facets of their sluggish and mundane existence.

Of course, I should be better at attaining and assimilating information about humans--after all, I used to be an integral part of one. Somehow, I was swept up into the biological creation of one of them, and I ended up composing much of its mental capabilities. This individual (*Anu* was the name given to him by his progenitors) was unaware of my presence simply because he did not have anything by which to gauge his perception. I was always with him, so he never knew anything different.

But that was millennia ago. So many generations of humanity have darted by since I have lost track of the lineage. For some time, I followed his descendants, possessing a somewhat overemotional parental complex over them. But watching them mature, mate, age, and die grew rather dull. It was depressing.

When humans are depressed, they emit a deep, pulsing psychic moan. I don't believe they are aware of it, but I can detect it. Sometimes, it is so irritating I have to zone out. By *zone out*, I mean leaving the general dimensional platform that contains the lamenting human. Platforms are easily transversed for me. Humans can do it, too. They just do not know it. At any given moment, humanity exists in at least a hundred different platforms, constantly bleeding from one to another. The differences are far too minute to be apparent to them. Humans are virtually blind.

A *generator* just walked in. That is a term I coined for certain humans (or certain members of many other species) which extend (willingly or unconsciously) their emotional states to others in relatively close proximity. Already, the four others in the chamber are being influenced by the generator. He is unknowingly forcing anger into them. Their heart rate quickens, blood pressure climbs, and muscles tense. It is all quite intriguing to observe.

Unfortunately, I do not have sufficient time to spend on such observation. I was sent with a purpose ... a purpose beyond observation, beyond clinical study. I have been trusted to interact with humans, to connect and control them if necessary. Such direct interference in the natural evolution of another species is normally frowned upon by my race; today, I do so with the approval of my superiors. I was the only one they could rely upon, the only one capable of such an important mission.

Until now, we have done our best not to disturb this species. Until now, intervention and contact were considered negligent, if not criminal. The liberal council governing the scattered civilization my race has nurtured has wisely chosen not to alarm humans with the knowledge of our coexistence. Further, studies have proven individual humans so utterly paranoid and violent that it is believed that by revealing ourselves, we would merely be providing the species with an additional target at which to aim their aggression. Humans have enough problems trying to keep from exterminating themselves.

Regardless of past traditions, we were separated races until now. Before, no one—human or otherwise—ever threatened our existence. Now, that has changed.

We have been monitoring one human intensely in the last passing instances of the continuum. As we watched, he went from childhood to adolescence and adulthood. These stages are structurally related to the life cycle stages of insects: larval, pupal, and adult.

During the adolescent period, this human cultivated means of projecting emotions willingly and learned to read other people's emotional and mental states. He also expanded his perceptual awareness of what most humans consider inanimate objects and elements of nature.

Initially, we thought he was the first trace of new progress in human evolution. We believed that humans were finally advancing beyond their physical form. But our expectations have been scuttled and our fears have been stirred.

The human named Anthony Quarta is the danger. We know that he has the power to obliterate the minds of every living thing on earth. And we also sense that he intends to utilize that power. His fellow man has become a mere nuisance to him. His power is too violent for him to control ... he no longer feels compassion, if he ever did, and the strain of his vast cognizance has left him with neither the time for or need of emotion. He is immersed in the constantly billowing reality he must define and store in memory. His consciousness has enveloped and absorbed so many alien emotions, so many lives and so many dimensions, that it has driven him insane. We assume.

We are giving him the benefit of our uncertainty. It is possible that he has, since conception, strove toward domination of the otherwise dormant capabilities humans possess. He may be more intelligent—and ambitious—than we believe. That would prove to be an additional hazard. If the situation is so critical that it warrants his immediate destruction, I am prepared to act.

To compound my problems, others of my kind (we, incidentally, refer to ourselves as relingan holomorphs) may be more anxious to destroy Anthony Quarta than I. Some feel he not only realizes what he is doing, and not only is he sane and unscrupulous, but his perceptual abilities and generator influences have already reached our domain. They claim that he is focusing images into we relingans. None of my studies imply he can image focus, yet many contend they have been witness and victim to such episodes.

If this is so, then I think nothing we could do could bother him. My mission, therefore, would be futile ... meaningless. Everything I think may be his thoughts. However, I tend to disagree with the theorists who have postulated this concept.

Or maybe, Anthony Quarta is making me disagree with it.

I am moving through the lighting fixtures in one of the main corridors of the human's multi-leveled structure. The paint on the walls is sliding down, sloping gracefully and fantastically slowly. Eventually, it will overwhelm the open area that the humans traverse. No, long before that, they will paint over and renew the process ... or knock the building down altogether.

Wooden doors buckled down with metal brackets and violated by metallic incisions mourn their baneful existence. Psychopathic air currents mix and twirl, form eddies, and die tragic spiral deaths. Delicate strands of moisture condense and huddle together in a stagnant corner. They are singing. Even without humans in its belly, a corridor can be deafening.

I sense Anthony Quarta ... nearby ... expelling emotions from someone. He is drawing an emotion out and replacing it ... with nothing. Normally, when pain is removed, the void is filled by instilling peace or pleasure. When fear is eradicated, courage replaces it. Anthony Quarta is erasing desire and leaving nothing in its place.

People who expel emotions as well as generate them are called *sublimators* or *healers*. I prefer the former because the latter is a word humans use for spiritualists who supposedly use a deity's power to take away pain or illness. Most of these healers are bogus ... some, who are actually sublimators, can perform their duty. But then, of course, they attribute the "miracle" to their deity.

I was unaware that Anthony Quarta was a sublimator, though it hardly surprised me. Casually, I enter the chamber where Anthony Quarta is presently existing. The atmosphere in the room thickens as I emerge from the wall; the texture of the air grows coarse. I ignore the minor alteration.

In the room with Anthony Quarta are three others ... all female, young, relatively unintelligent, and unhealthy. One of them has a small, cancerous tumor on her cerebrum. It has not yet begun to affect her adversely, but it will lead to her extinction. Anthony Quarta is communicating verbally with this individual. It was toward her that his sublimating skills were directed. He apparently selected not to extinguish the cancer—though he is aware of it and it is within his power to dispel it. He is aware of the thoughts of each of these women, thoughts of which these women themselves may not be aware. Their memories are his. Their hopes and their dreams are his. Their nightmares, too, are his. His mind seems flooded. Overloaded. Too many thoughts, ideas, values, wishes, fears, sorrows, triumphs, failures, regrets, aspirations, impressions, conceits, convictions, views, prejudices, doubts, needs...

STATIC.

There is no possibility that he could contain so much. Those of my race are able to focus our intake and filter it. Monitor it. Cease to acquire it when we are burdened. He does not have this luxury. Yet, he continues, grasping at the pieces of mental static that litter this chamber. He imbibes all that IS these women ... and does so with every tangible being and unliving object within at least a hundred-mile radius. He flirts with insanity. He taunts it.

He invites it.

He could wipe these peoples' minds clean. It would be a simple, almost thoughtless task. They would merely expire, and he would move on.

As if in response to my pondering, Anthony Quarta clears the three women of every grain of thought and memory in their heads. They forget their names, their lives, their experience. They forget families, husbands, and children. They forget dressing like Caspar the Ghost on Halloween; making uncomfortable, sweaty love in a Datsun B210; watching a two-year-old playing with an orange kitten just brought home from the kennel. They forget to breathe and pump blood.

Death.

They are his first victims. I must see that they are his final victims as well.

I move toward him, flinging myself at his warping mind. In a second, he has committed the same atrocity upon every human in that hundred-mile radius. He knows. He knows I am there and have been sent to stop him. Now, he taunts me. He mocks me.

He invites me...

Does he want to be stopped? Perhaps there is compassion curled in an embryonic ball deep within his brain. Regardless, I continue toward him, penetrate his flesh, and dive into his mind.

I am not alone.

Besides me ... besides Anthony Quarta ... there are others. My kind. Relingan holo-morphs. We are shackled.

Anthony Quarta has lured us here. He is using my kind to multiply his powers. He is using us as storage tanks for his perception. And we are powerless to revolt, warn others, or do anything. He will soon be open and alive to areas of awareness that even my kind never recognized.

Soon, he will be the sole reality.

All that will exist is Anthony Quarta—and that which he creates within his mind.

The End

The Lynchin' Tree by Lee Clark Zumpe

When they built the courthouse
during Reconstruction,
that old oak already had a reputation.

Now, some folks used to post bulletins –
nail 'em right to the trunk,
legal notices, wanted posters and such.

Might be mentioned that in its shade
plantation owners once gathered,
inspecting new shipments from African shores.

And then there was Augustus:
a mob dragged him from the jailhouse,
set him to swinging for something next to nothing.

Been four summers since lightning struck it,
its twisted branches blackened
and leaves scattered like severed digits.

Dead and rotted, they cut it down –
But when the moon wills it,
I still see the shadow of the lynchin' tree.

In The Shadows by Kendall Evans

You lurk in bloodred shadows
Cloaked in shrouding darkness—
And you languorously drink your fill
From innocent passers-by

IT CAME FROM INSIDE THE INKWELL!   By Vincent Davis

"THAT'S NOT JUST ANY CREEPY MAN LOOKING IN OUR WINDOW SON!
IT'S NICOLAS CAGE!"

The Golden Hour
by
Rod Marsden

In memory of Jack Kirby, the best American artist of the 20th century and also in memory of Gene Colan, American artist and photographer.

There is a time just before the sun sets that photographers call the golden hour. It lasts less than an hour and is easily missed. Looking through the lens during this time, one can see the world light up, and subjects glow with peculiar energy. When something unexpected happened, Jack Hines photographed a black-shouldered kite in a tree near Fairy Meadow, south of Sydney. There was the expected glow, also the bird, but there was something else. The figure of a young woman in a white gown with wings flittered past, and her image was captured on his digital camera. What did it mean? What could it mean?

Jack tried showing the photograph to his friends and family, but the girl with the wings was there only for him. All anyone else saw was a predatory bird atop a pine tree. Both the bird and the tree glowed golden, but that was it. Jack was old and knew his time on Earth was almost up. The face of what he now thought of as an angel was blank and emotionless. He wondered why.

Was there something he could do or should do before he died? Jack had money. In his will; there was money for his children and a large amount for the birds and animals in the wilderness areas of New South Wales. He believed in preserving the habitats of endangered species. He wanted the platypus and birds, such as the black-shouldered kite, to always have a place in his Australia.

Nothing was magical about the black-shouldered kite, a large white bird with black shoulder feathers that preyed on lizards and snakes. On the other hand, the platypus was so unlikely that it took some effort to convince those in the London Museum to agree that the creature was not some hoax. Added to this is the shyness of the platypus and Jack's desire to someday see one in the wild. Unfortunately, this desire was never fulfilled.

People considered Jack eccentric for caring about birds, but this did not faze him. His wife passed away years ago, and now he loved his family, friends, and the wild places where he took his camera. He once laughed at his image in a service station mirror of an elderly man out on the hunt with his camera. His trophies were the best pictures he had taken of the creatures he loved. He put them on his wall at home in Wollongong to be admired by himself and visitors. The angel, however, would not go on his wall. She could be transferred from camera to computer but could only be viewed by him.

Jack sometimes wondered why people put dead things on their walls. It was popular in England and Scotland during the 18th and 19th centuries, and Americans still do it in the 21st century. He knew he would be haunted and not in a good way if he had a moose's head on one of his walls. Jack loved the notion that the creatures he photographed were still alive. Killing for the sport, he thought, was sick, but he could go along with killing for food. He was not a vegetarian.

Then, events overtook Jack. Israel was attacked, and days later, people were on the steps to the Sydney Opera House calling out to gas the Jews. Time passed, and more hate was displayed.

The Prime Minister did little to help against this. People like Jack had lived peaceful, productive lives in Australia for over seventy years. Jack and others were born in Sydney, and their parents were survivors of the holocaust. When a synagogue was destroyed, images of Crystal Night in Germany came to him together with the words on the opera house steps to gas the Jews. Why were decent, good-hearted Australians letting this happen again? Why did decent, good-hearted Germans allow such horror to occur in the first place long ago?

Buddhists living south of Wollongong, New South Wales, in Unanderra, were in sympathy with those Jews who had had their synagogue destroyed in Melbourne. There were also Catholic and Protestant groups who agreed that the burning of a place of worship should never have happened in Australia. These people loved, not hated. He recalled reading about a Lutheran preacher in Germany who, before the Second World War, spoke out against the mistreatment of Jews.

But what could Jack do? It had been years since he had visited his synagogue near Hurstville, and he didn't consider himself religious. He had been a successful store owner who mostly sold toys. When it was time to retire, he had given the business to his son. Now, he knew he was dying of cancer, and his days were numbered. Even so, the wilderness still called out for whatever help he could muster. His photos were sometimes published in magazines, letting people know what was still out there and needed humanity's protection.

Now, Jack wanted revenge on those once again calling out for blood. Should he send money to an Israeli military organisation for weapons to aid them in their fight against the forces that would destroy Israel? No. He had not been a violent man. He had sold toys to children and would hate himself if he were in any way responsible for more violence. What was left? What could he do if he did not add to the bloodshed and destruction? He felt so helpless against the rising tide of hate. Where had it come from? Had the federal government imported too many people with hatred in their hearts? In Germany, Christians could no longer be safe at Christmas, and the same was true in New Orleans, USA, around Christmas time. Was the whole world going insane?

Jack shrugged and headed out to Wollongong Botanic Garden with camera in hand. There, he came upon a male and female bower bird bathing in the birdbath near the entrance. They appeared to be having a jolly time splashing about. The male bowerbird was dark blue, and the female green. According to other birders, Jack knew he was supposed to find the male more attractive, but he loved the fierceness of the female in all her green glory. For a while, he forgot his cares and his need to make those who had destroyed a place of worship more accountable for their actions. He took pictures. It then came to him that this area, and many like it, were his places of worship. Here, among these birds, he could find his God. It was quite a revelation.

A week later, Jack visited his lawyer and created a new will. He did not change the amount he would give his children but the amount he would pass on to the wilderness society to protect his beloved wildlife. He put aside an amount for the rebuilding of the synagogue in Melbourne. This was his idea of revenge. It might not stop the hate, but it was a stand. He might never revisit a synagogue, but that was all right. Replacing burnt books in Melbourne might not be possible, so some damage was irreversible. Even so, no lives were lost this time, which was a blessing. The same could not be said against Christianity regarding recent events in Germany and New Orleans, USA.

Moving away from hate and to thoughts of rebuilding the synagogue, which was more important to other Jews, made him feel good. Jack looked at the photo of the angel for the last time. He was surprised to find a smile on her face. Had he done something to put the smile there? Moments later, he passed away. As he did so, the glow of the golden hour engulfed him. What a perfect time to leave the world, his family, friends, and beloved birds and animals.

The End

In the Hollywood Hills by Sandy DeLuca

Anna gathers fallen branches from the field;
white hands long and slender,
olden trailer beneath
the gibbous moon—
Santa Monica Mountains along the
Pacific—
wildfires burn in the distance.

Wanderers, cons and freaks
traveled East long ago—
left her alone beneath the redwoods.

Remnants come and go;
feathers from the snake lady's boa
and a ticket smeared with mud.

Float away—
ghosts for a hundred Octobers—
like bones beneath the earth.

A silver voice calls to her—
a black-clad man beyond
the border of life and death—
lights flicker, and cards
spread over lace cloth—
two pieces of silver and three
one-dollar bills.

She gazes at him
through the mist,
then turns away...

She always does.

No time for parlor tricks,
or a grand entrance for those
who yearn to learn secrets
from beyond the grave.

She drifts to a darkened
highway where she makes crosses
tied with sewing thread,
places them along the road--
plaster flowers and beads
for praying
wrapped around splintered wood

Trucks rush past her
spraying mud
and autumn rain—

She raises her arms
to the sky—
unseen to most;
just a whisper—
longing for the caravan
to take her home.

Diet or Die
by
Matthew Wilson

It was rude to ask about woman's weight, but my doctor insists a diet was necessary, though obesity has always been in my family, and Halloween is only days away—it would be wrong to drop traditions now. But I have become too big for my broom, and chasing children is getting harder.

I am not one to waste food or leave survivors.

Must a witch watch her waistline? Counting calories is no life for such a creature, but I may have been too greedy lately. Too many missing children brings unwanted attention, but it *is* almost Halloween and it would be a shame to let anyone escape my candy house.

Yes, the doctor is right. For my health, I really need to lose a few stones.

But first, I will have my Halloween treats.

And maybe a few children roasting on the spit for Christmas dinner.

The End

My Sister's Shell by Matthew Wilson

At night, my sister comes to the window
My sibling with a deep sense of play
But mother would scream if she saw her
Since we put her coffin down in the clay.
Sylvia was the eldest and the adventurer
The one who told me to always be brave
So of course, she was first and firm
When we dared to the old Baron's grave.
Even dead men it seems hate intruders
And I ran when his talons pierced the ground
Sylvia pushed me from the shadow of his cape
Then he swept her away with hardly a sound.
It has been years since mother called a coward
But not as long as I returned to that place
A man exhuming that bastard Baron's coffin
And spitting holy water on his sleeping face.
Still at night my sister comes to the window
Telling me stories of how she rules the skies
And how I hate myself for still loving her
Even though she has lost the life within her eyes.

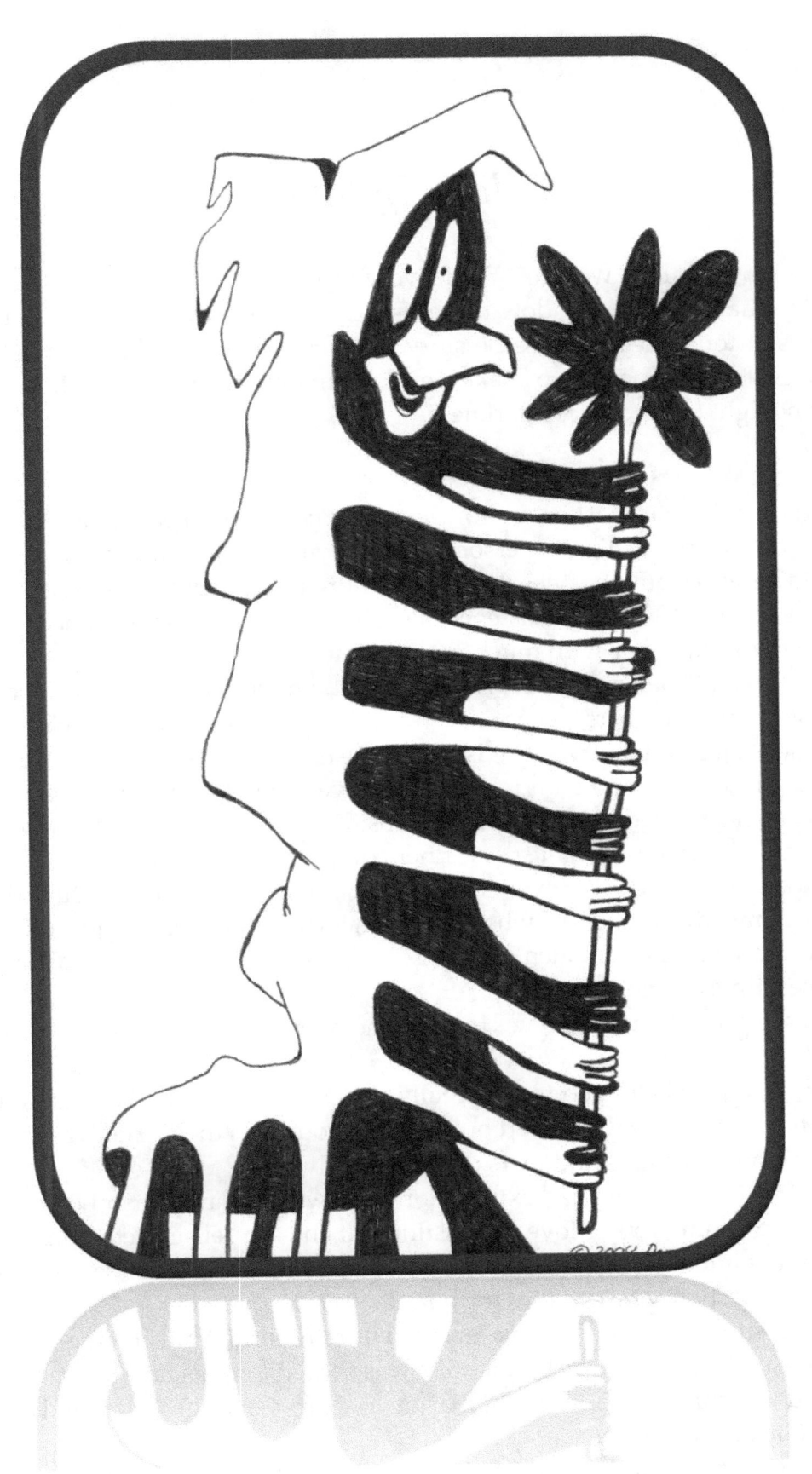

In Widow's Weeds
by
Hillary Lyon

A young widow's tale of woe gets them every time.

Never mind that the young widow has been bereaved for several generations, that the great-grandfathers of today heard the same story from her rose-tinted lips. Lips that curved down ever so slightly, just enough to make her companions wonder how they—and they alone—could bring light to her morose darkness.

So it goes.

****

Eva joined an online support group for the newly bereaved. It was to her liking; it was much better than the groups meeting in person. How tedious and tiresome the in-person group sessions tended to be, especially the ones that met in church fellowship halls. All those crosses, hymnals, and prayer books! The very existence of such things turned her stomach.

The internet provided her with much more freedom.

She learned to craft personas that would draw the most attention and sincerest sympathy from online group members—especially from the group's curators. In video sessions, she wore authentic Victorian widow's weeds; everyone else wore their everyday clothes and looked depressed, disheveled, and bland. Eva looked every inch the solemn angel in mourning, with her pale skin and black hair, her carved obsidian heart pendant nesting against her full bosom, and her knack for posing *just so* for her computer's tiny camera.

All eyes were drawn to Eva, even when other members had the virtual floor. And though it was discouraged, members sent her private messages. Messages requesting meetings over coffee, meetings over a casual lunch, meetings in the park—just for conversation, for mutual support in their time of grief.

Of course, she said yes, yes, and yes to each and every one.

****

Each grief group she belonged to eventually closed down as members drifted away—often without notice. A few always moved on to other groups, as their grief was never extinguished, and they craved the ears and tears of other survivors.

Eva felt otherwise. Her grief had expired long ago with the internment of her first husband, Jonathan. He'd promised her love everlasting but chose a self-inflicted death over living with her. She was attending the theater when it happened; she never saw his body and never had the opportunity to prepare him for burial.

At that time, suicides didn't receive proper church burials, but having come from a wealthy and well-established line, the young man was settled into his family's mausoleum—an ornately carved structure inspired by the Parthenon, large enough inside to host several deceased generations. Which it did.

His family did not appear shocked by his untimely death. They celebrated, instead, with a grand wake. There was much feasting on rare meats and toasting with obscure red wines. A blindfolded quartet played curious chamber music, songs from the "old country," as one ancient black-laced and jet-beaded *grande* dame informed her. Eva was hailed by the family as the belle of the ball. She danced until her feet bled.

On the first anniversary of Jonathan's passing, Eva paid a visit to his tomb, which was his family's custom; for although they were married a brief time, his kin still embraced her as family since he had chosen her from all the eligible women in his orbit to be his bride. Alone in the growing twilight, dressed still in her widow's weeds, Eva laid roses on the cold stone lid of his sarcophagus, softly hummed hymns (as she had forgotten the words), lit candles, murmured prayers and, as she had been instructed by the family, waited—waited for the rough scraping of stone against stone as the lid was shoved aside, waited for Jonathan to arise and bestow upon her the kiss he had promised her before his death. A kiss to solve all her problems and bind them together forever.

She didn't have to wait long.

****

Jonathan, liberated from his tomb, embraced Eva roughly and took from her what he craved. As he still felt a fondness for Eva, he left enough of her essence for her to survive. She collapsed onto the floor of the tomb, weakly reaching for him, begging for answers to the questions that pained her soul— "Why did you leave me? Was our life together so awful?"

He laughed. "Need I point out that human life in general is awful? You shouldn't be so self-centered," he added coldly. "You had little to nothing to do with my choice; I am following the family way."

"But what shall I do now?" she cried out, full to the brim with fear and panic. "Where shall I go?"

Jonathan belched, wiped his mouth with the back of his hand, and replied flippantly, "You're a bright girl; you'll figure it out." He then flashed his handsome wolfish grin—the one that won her heart in the first place—bowed deeply, thanked her, and bade Eva goodbye. He was gone before she could rise from the hard-packed earthen floor of the sepulcher, before she could grab the hem of his grave clothes to stop him, before she could remind him he'd promised they'd be together forever. Ravaged and abandoned! Eva wept until she was dry. Long after midnight, she wiped her tear-streaked face, brushed the dirt from her widow's weeds, and shambled home, a ghost of her former self.

All subsequent suitors and mates were merely amusements, salves to her eternal boredom. Soft-hearted sustenance to satiate her appetite.

****

Eva traveled from city to city—it was easy to attract suitors in a big city. She created fictitious backgrounds for herself, and the men, smitten by her charm and beauty, never asked the questions that would knock down the scaffolds supporting her stories. Frontier towns were fun, too, as the men she found there were sincere and desperate for love. And anywhere during wartime was lovely, as young men on leave from the battlefield were, emotionally, such easy prey.

Then the modern world arrived, mewling and kicking like a newborn brat. Eva wasn't too keen on women's liberation; now, she had competition from other females for the male gaze. Many women gleefully showed a bit of fish-netted thigh, flashed a bit of cleavage in the latest fashion of low-necked frocks, and painted their lips with alluring glosses. Hippy chicks were the worst, giving away entrance to their private chambers without consideration of remuneration or reputation.

And so, the decades scrolled by.

Recently, a plague landed Eva in the best of times—lockdowns and self-isolation provided her with the tools for curated access to her charms. The computer camera loved her, and the cell phone camera loved her; she was irresistible on the small screens, and she knew it. Women's fashion had circled around to the point that anyone could wear anything, and no one commented nor cared. So Eva once again donned her beloved widow's weeds.

And hunting was easier than ever.

Since Jonathan couldn't be bothered to teach her what to do and how to do it, Eva—who had always considered herself to be self-sufficient—did, in fact, "figure it out." And what a bullet she had dodged when Jonathan fled, abandoning her on that cold earthen floor; a silver bullet, as she now jokingly phrased it to herself.

What had become of the cruelly selfish Jonathan, anyway? Decades ago, Eva came across a newspaper article about a man—a darkly handsome man who greatly resembled Jonathan in the grainy black and white picture on the front page—who had been arrested for serial killing. This man was to be electrocuted down in Florida in the crude wooden chair that the press fondly referred to as "Old Sparky." It appears that somewhere along the way, Jonathan had changed his name to Ted.

She didn't mourn his final demise. You must understand, she confided to me over coffee; it's hard to mend a broken heart after that heart has compressed into a cold black stone by decades of unrelenting, wounded rage. And even when you've had that heart-stone set in a 24K gold filigreed pendant, and you wear it every day for all eternity, there is no relief; it never warms. It still hurts.

The End

To Wed a Vampire by Marge Simon

She shares a legacy of death and blood,
Knows she will be spared no mercy,
Humiliated by false gossip,
Accused of inhuman acts,
Not by her own volition.

But at her wedding
She wears a gown of bombazine,
A bouquet of barbed wire
In her bleeding hands.

A pale man in black waits
At an altar draped in scarlet.
The Undead gathered bow their heads
Whispering dark hosannas
When the ceremony ends.

Night Gallery

Day Shift

Review by Lee Clark Zumpe

In vampire film "Day Shift," action supersedes horror and comedy

Some people prefer their horror with a hint of humor — or their comedy with a helping of horror. Those who fall into either subcategory can express their deepest gratitude, and should they desire, make ritual offerings to one of the so-called *Lads of Kilkenny* and founder of the literary journal *Salmagundi*. In those youthful days, the author employed such colorful pseudonyms such as William Wizard and Launcelot Langstaff. Most of those who didn't sleep through their literature classes will recognize his actual name: Washington Irving.

Irving has been credited by some as the first author to blend horror and humor in one of his most famous short stories. "The Legend of Sleepy Hollow," published in 1820, is part campfire ghost story, part gothic tale, and part burlesque. Ichabod Crane, desperate in his desire to marry Katrina Van Tassel, mocks the typical romantic hero. He is a gawky, gangly, easily unsettled schoolmaster with a tendency to gossip and an irrational fear of ghosts, goblins, and witchcraft. His interest in the 18-year-old Van Tassel has more to do with her family's wealth and influence than any starry-eyed notions of love. His rival for Katrina's affections takes advantage of his superstitious nature, culminating in the disappearance of Crane from Sleepy Hollow after a late-night chase involving the alleged ghost of a headless Hessian soldier. The story is simultaneously scary and silly. It has the ability to make you shiver and giggle, like any good Halloween yarn.

Victor Frankenstein himself — fictitious master of constructing life out of mismatched jigsaw puzzle pieces plucked from graveyards — could not have imagined all the myriad ways in which filmmakers would mix, mingle, and meld comedy and horror. In 1948, *Abbott and Costello Meet Frankenstein* paired one of the most popular comedy duos of the era with some of the leading stars of Universal Studios Monsters franchise, including Lon Chaney Jr. and Bela Lugosi. Bud Abbott and Lou Costello did several additional films in this vein, including *Abbott and Costello Meet the Killer, Boris Karloff, Abbott and Costello Meet the Invisible Man, Abbott and Costello Meet Dr. Jekyll and Mr. Hyde,* and *Abbott and Costello Meet the Mummy.*

But Abbott and Costello weren't the first to tap into the horror-comedy mashup.

As early as 1917, filmmakers were finding ways to combine laughter and screams, such as in the German silent film *The Golem and the Dancing Girl,* which is sadly now considered a lost film. Walt Disney even took a stab at the horror spoof with the 1929 animated short *The Haunted House,* featuring Mickey Mouse.

Prior to 1970, most attempts at blending horror and comedy tipped the scales in favor of humor. The filmmakers routinely opted for campy, silly scares rather than scream-inducing terror or buckets of blood and gore. In the 1970s, a few moviemakers tossed the old recipe book and started from scratch.

For modern audiences, films such as *The Abominable Dr. Phibes* (1971), *Young Frankenstein* (1974), *The Return of the Living Dead* (1985), *The Lost Boys* (1987), *Army of Darkness* (1992), *The Frighteners* (1996), *Shaun of the Dead* (2004), and *Zombieland* (2009) have come to define the quirky, unpredictable subgenre.

Day Shift is a new addition to the field. This horror-comedy vampire romp was released on Netflix Aug. 12, 2022.

In *Day Shift*, Jamie Foxx stars as blue-collar dad Bud Jablonski, whose San Fernando Valley pool cleaning job is a clever ruse to hide his actual occupation. Bud hunts vampires. He's good at it, too, but he apparently has issues with following the rules, which put him at odds with the vampire hunting union, his former employer. At the beginning of the story, he is freelancing: Killing vampires in the daytime as they sleep and extracting their fangs, which he can sell to a black-market dealer in a local pawnshop.

When Bud learns that his estranged wife Jocelyn (Meagan Good) plans on selling the house and relocating to Florida with their daughter Paige (Zion Broadnax) because of financial issues, he vows to earn enough money to convince her to stay in California.

Bud turns to fellow vampire hunter Big John (Snoop Dogg), who helps him get reinstated in the union. Seeger (Eric Lange), the new union boss, only allows it so that he can catch Bud breaking the rules and prohibit him from the union for all time. He assigns Seth (Dave Franco)—a gawky, gangly, easily unsettled union rep—to babysit Bud, knowing the pencil-pusher will make note of every code violation and report it.

In trying to make a living, Bud manages to enrage Audrey (Karla Souza), the most dangerous vampire in Southern California and a real estate mogul. Audrey already has big plans: She speaks of a time in history when humans worshiped vampires as gods, and she's looking to start a war to Make Vampires Great Again. Nevertheless, she finds time to torment Bud by abducting Jocelyn and Paige, which leads to an inevitable showdown.

Perry is an American martial artist, action director, actor, and stuntman. The hype promoting *Day Shift* emphasizes the fact that it while it may be a horror film, it's also received a healthy transfusion of gritty action. That bodybuilding supplement comes from 87North Productions, the production company behind *John Wick, Nobody, Atomic Blonde,* and *Bullet Train.* So, in addition to blending horror and comedy, *Day Shift* adds an element of high-speed, blood-spattered action featuring intense fight choreography and brutal slugfests. That means Perry has to cover a lot of territory in his efforts at world-building, character development, and storytelling.

Maybe that's why *Day Shift* doesn't feel as immersive as it should. The constant tonal shifts make it difficult to connect on an emotional level with Bud and his cohorts. The scenes with Bud and his daughter are promising, but the script is so focused on action that it fails to develop their relationship fully. The same is true of the quirky bond that forms between Bud and Seth. Two minor characters—the hardcore vampire-hunting Nazarian brothers played by Steve Howey and Scott Adkins—have already generated a cult following, with viewers asking when they will get their own movie.

It's a case of there's so much of everything, there's not enough of anything: There's not enough Snoop Dogg; there's not enough of Franco's nerdy, bumbling Seth; there's not enough of Foxx's well-intentioned but cocky gallantry; and there's definitely not enough focus on the family dynamic to provide the groundwork for any kind of reconciliation.

Day Shift is also lacking in another area—and this is important if you're here for the horror: It's not scary. The vampires are narcissistic, pompous, and self-indulgent. Audrey is more megalomaniacal Bond villain than menacing uber vampire.

While the movie isn't a complete washout, it's a shame that it feels so incomplete. The cast is outstanding, the action scenes are gripping, and the story is fun and engrossing. It just doesn't quite manage to sink its teeth into the viewer. It generates more superficial smiles than hearty guffaws. Its breakneck pace during vampire attack scenes leaves no time for terror.

Perry clearly admires the horror-comedy subgenre.

"I'm a big fan of *Big Trouble in Little China, The Lost Boys,* and the original *Fright Night,*" Perry said in the film's production notes. "I'm 53 so I loved the action-comedy-horror movies from the '80s. It's a genre that feels like it's almost been forgotten. Like, a film like *Zombieland* was cool, but it's not as common as it used to be. A film is either action or comedy or horror. I think combining them like this is a lot more fun. I also think getting a laugh out of somebody right now is going to go a lot further than upsetting them by making them dive into some deep dark story."

By putting too much emphasis on the action component, *Day Shift* is only intermittently entertaining, leaving the viewer with a handful of rousing action sequences scattered across a mostly forgettable landscape populated with under-developed characters and materialistic vampires.

The vampires of Santa Carla and Sunnydale are far more interesting.

Lee Clark Zumpe is entertainment editor at Tampa Bay Newspapers, a Tomatometer-Approved Critic, and an author of short fiction appearing in select anthologies and magazines. Follow Lee at www.patreon.com/Haunter_of_the_Bijou.

Fresh

Review by Lee Clark Zumpe

The pitfalls of dating serve as a springboard to macabre horror in "Fresh."

Thankfully, I haven't had to contemplate the rigors of the dating scene for more than 20 years. Even in the late 1990s, it was no picnic—unless you happen to like a challenge and select an actual picnic as a first-date stratagem for someone you met online, in a bar, or through a real-world social network such as church, professional associations, community organizations, fitness centers, or support groups. For someone with social anxiety, initiating any new relationship is strenuous and exhausting. The more you think about all the things that could go wrong, the more terrifying it seems.

The dating scene can be perceived as a nightmarish wasteland populated by toxic narcissists, condescending misogynists, and other assorted sociopaths—and that makes it the perfect backdrop for modern horror cinema.

In recent years, breakout filmmakers have delivered a steady stream of horror movies revolving around toxic relationships. These are the antithesis of the rom-com: They are designed to critique the psychology of modern dating and make viewers reflect upon the interpersonal processes that are in play as a relationship develops. The films cover everything from meeting the parents (see *Get Out,* 2017) and shared holidays (see *Midsommar,* 2019) to dealing with children from prior marriages (see *The Lodge,* 2020) and full-throttle, hardcore obsession (see *Pet,* 2016).

Joining this pack of films that capitalize on the apprehension and vulnerability that comes with dating is *Fresh,* the directorial debut for Mimi Cave. The film was released March 4, 2022, on Hulu by Searchlight Pictures.

The film opens with a vignette depicting what appears to be a worst-case first-date scenario: Noa (Daisy Edgar-Jones) meets Chad (Brett Dier) for dinner at a Chinese restaurant, where he talks about his acid reflux, criticizes her clothing and her appearance, makes her pay for both their meals, and commandeers her leftovers for himself. It goes downhill from there—but, at least Chad's unpleasantness never amounts to anything more than the whiny chauvinism of a malcontent deadbeat.

After discussing the pitfalls of dating apps with her friend Mollie (Jonica T. Gibbs), Noa has a chance meeting with Steve (Sebastian Stan) at a grocery store. She finds his awkward humor charming, and he convinces her to give him her number. They connect over the course of a few dates, and Steve invites her to run off with him for a romantic weekend getaway. The destination, he tells her, is a surprise.

Red flag, anyone?

This is where *Fresh* does something that's—well, fresh. Up until this point, approximately 30 minutes into the film, the script could have been heading in a number of different directions. Comedy, romance, drama—any one of these paths could have been possible. Shortly after Noa and Steve arrive at their destination, the bottom drops out and, around the 33-minute mark, the film's opening credits appear onscreen.

What transpires over the remaining 80 minutes of running time is a provocative, grotesque feast of decadence and an attack on entitlement. Going into too much detail would spoil the film's puzzles, so I'll only provide as much information as the studio supplies in its official synopsis: Noa discovers "her new paramour has been hiding some unusual appetites."

While the story may not be entirely original, the way Cave presents it certainly feels jarringly inventive. Despite the macabre subject matter, *Fresh* often employs wickedly depraved humor and sporadically shifts tone, moving from the ghastly to the absurd in a heartbeat. Cave shrewdly misleads, subverts, and destabilizes: She utterly macerates audience expectations and topples a few sacred cows along the way. Her feminist approach is neither preachy nor self-righteous, though the film takes its time revealing a single male character who isn't awful.

The vigilant viewer will spot more than one occasion in which Noa does something particularly rash or irresponsible. She is not immune to making bad decisions that exacerbate the dilemma. Edgar-Jones plays the complex part exceedingly well, particularly considering the fact that she must fluctuate between fawning lover and tenacious survivor.

Stan's portrayal of Steve is unnerving and sinister. Even during the first 30 minutes of setup and misdirection, Stan manages to slip in traces of loathsomeness beneath Steve's swagger and charm.

Fresh is a stylish, uncompromising, and surprisingly artistic depiction of endemic exploitation, the ubiquity of toxic masculinity, and perseverance. It is twisted and unsettling, and equally capable of eliciting a smile and a laugh as well as a wince and a shudder. Certainly not meant for the squeamish, *Fresh* is a transgressive treat with a sharp feminist perspective.

Lee Clark Zumpe is entertainment editor at Tampa Bay Newspapers, a Tomatometer-Approved Critic, and an author of short fiction appearing in select anthologies and magazines. Follow Lee at www.patreon.com/Haunter_of_the_Bijou.

Hatching

Review by Lee Clark Zumpe

Finnish horror film "Hatching" is a cryptic coming-of-age dark fantasy.

Guess what: Parenting is hard. It's not for the squeamish. It can undermine your financial stability, complicate relationships, and gut you emotionally. Expect an array of sleepless nights, costly emergency room visits, and schoolyard skirmishes involving vicious bullies. Unless you're very fortunate, don't expect a village—seems like everyone is either too exhausted or too preoccupied with checking off boxes on their bucket lists to lend a hand these days.

Parenting is hard—and absolutely worth all the fatigue, worry, and heartbreak. It is as terrifying at times as it is rewarding. And even though our species has had thousands of years to perfect the art of childrearing, somehow it seems each succeeding generation stumbles around blindly trying to reinvent the wheel. It's been a few years, but I still remember attending the mandatory classes at the hospital where our daughter was born, covering the birth process, breastfeeding, and newborn care. I remember the *What to Expect* books cluttering the coffee table in the living room. I remember that we both shambled around like zombies for the first three months due to lack of sleep. I also remember that my daughter had slept through the first seven seasons of *CSI* before she was 3 months old.

If parenting is hard for those going into the endeavor with the best intentions, imagine what it must be like for those who haven't really thought it through properly. There are books dedicated to outlining toxic, dysfunctional forms of parenting. Some parents demand perfection in every arena from the first day of preschool, while others want to live vicariously through the achievements of their child. Some remove all obstacles so that their child is never challenged. Helicopter parents micromanage every minute of their children's lives, while the laissez-faire parent avoids any form of guidance and discipline.

A new Finnish body horror film revolves around a highly dysfunctional family led by a narcissistic mother who puts her personal pursuits over her children's best interests. *Hatching*—or *Pahanhautoja* in the original tongue—is directed by Hanna Bergholm and written by Ilja Rautsi. The cast includes Jani Volanen, Reino Nordin, Saija Lentonen, Siiri Solalinna and Sophia Heikkilä. The film was released in select theaters and on demand April 29, 2022, through IFC Midnight.

In the film, Tinja (Solalinna), a young gymnast, tries desperately to please her mother (Heikkilä), a woman obsessed with presenting the image of a perfect family life to the whole world through her popular vlog. After an incident in which a crow flies into the family's home and damages the interior décor, Tinja finds a strange egg in the forest behind the house. She hides it, keeps it warm, and nurtures it as it gets bigger and bigger. When it finally hatches, what emerges is a nightmarish bird-monster. With ghastly, oversized eyes, this slimy, bony creature dotted by an occasional tuft of gray feathers both repels and captivates Tinja.

More than a standard creature-feature flick, *Hatching* satirizes the tawdriness of influencer culture and social media façades. Tinja's mother fixates on presenting a portrait of perfection to her audience, choreographing every aspect of this suburban nuclear family as if arranging them in a doll house. From the very beginning of the film when the crow flies through the open door, chaos starts to chip away at that carefully constructed veneer.

Simultaneously, *Hatching* sees Tinja transfer all her coming-of-age anxieties into the egg. It feeds on her insecurity, her frustration, and her desperate need to live up to her mother's expectations. Once the thing hatches, the psychic link between the two only grows stronger. While Tinja continues to present herself as the perfect daughter her mother envisions, the creature—feral and lacking any moral compass—acts out the pent-up aggression and hostility Tinja has repressed.

But the creature isn't necessarily evil. It acts instinctively, unconstrained by any code of ethics. Like Tinja, it craves affection.

The body horror components in *Hatching* are clearly influenced by David Cronenberg. Hardcore horror fans may also be reminded of *Basket Case,* a low-budget film written and directed by Frank Henenlotter. The theme also evokes George Romero's *Monkey Shines.*

Hatching is perfectly capable of making viewers squirm. It is unsettling and frequently repulsive. The creature design and execution stand out as the film's most impressive achievements. Opting for an animatronic puppet instead of CGI, the director tapped Gustav Hoegen, known for his work on *Jurassic World: Fallen Kingdom,* 2010's *Clash of the Titan,* as well as components of the *Star Wars* franchise. Special effects make-up used in *Hatching* came from Academy Award-nominated effects artist Conor O'Sullivan.

Something about the film feels unfinished. The allegory it seeks to present never fully coalesces. It may be that some of the film's impact is lost in translation, particularly in terms of convincing viewers to empathize with Tinja. A high-concept fairy tale punctuated by moments that are legitimately shocking and revolting, *Hatching* can't quite reconcile its satirical and subversive elements with the blood-and-gore violence that increases as the creature completes its metamorphosis.

Meticulously polished and stylish, *Hatching* may garner a cult following for its fanciful grotesqueness even though it seems to be as perplexed about what it wants to be as its central character.

Lee Clark Zumpe is entertainment editor at Tampa Bay Newspapers, a Tomatometer-Approved Critic, and an author of short fiction appearing in select anthologies and magazines. Follow Lee at www.patreon.com/Haunter_of_the_Bijou.

Hellraiser

Review by Lee Clark Zumpe

Fittingly gory and gruesome, "Hellraiser" reenergizes franchise.

Let me start with an acknowledgment: Clive Barker changed the direction of my life. He is one of many authors whose work provided inspiration and motivation in my younger years as I sought direction as an aspiring writer.

By 1987, I knew I wanted to be a storyteller—to create interesting and compelling characters, build expansive worlds, develop an expanding mythos and generally spin a ripping good yarn. I also had a fascination with horror, thanks to genre heavyweights such as Edgar Allan Poe and H.P. Lovecraft. While I appreciated the inventiveness in the style and themes of Poe and Lovecraft, neither offered a practical template for approaching modern audiences.

Then I discovered Barker's short fiction.

Barker came to prominence in the 1980s with a series of short story collections published in six volumes known as *Books of Blood*. I still own my original paperback set, published by Berkley Books. Each volume is ragged and dog-eared.

The first book in the series, featured an introduction by Ramsey Campbell, followed by the first tale: *The Book of Blood*. This volume also included *The Midnight Meat Train, The Yattering and Jack, Pig Blood Blues, Sex, Death and Starshine,* and finally, the unforgettable story *In the Hills, the Cities.*

The first volume of *Books of Blood* was printed in 1984 and the final in 1985. Barker's work was unlike anything I had previously encountered in horror. It was bold and bleak. It was passionate and exacting. It was ugly and beautiful. It was new blood: an unencountered strain of dark, viral literature.

Barker's *Books of Blood* revealed the depth and impact of well-written modern short horror stories. The quality of his work provided a level of virtuosity to which I continue to aspire.

Like many, I became aware of Barker thanks to the 1987 British horror film *Hellraiser,* which was based on his 1986 novella *The Hellbound Heart.* Barker wrote the screenplay and directed the adaptation. It brought the Cenobites to the big screen, introduced the world at large to Pinhead, and spawned nine sequels—the most recent being *Hellraiser: Judgment,* released in 2018.

I won't bother to detail how disappointing most of these sequels have been.

Now, *Hellraiser* is back in a brand-new reinvention of Barker's 1987 horror classic. Directed by David Bruckner, the new film was released exclusively on Hulu as a Hulu original film Oct. 7, 2022.

In this version, Riley (Odessa A'zion) is struggling with a drug addiction. Homeless and couch surfing, she has settled in a small room in an apartment shared by her brother Matt (Brandon Flynn) and his boyfriend Colin (Adam Faison), as well as their roommate Nora (Aoife Hinds). Riley is dating Trevor (Drew Starkey), a fellow recovering addict she met in a 12-step program.

An introductory scene set several years before the events depicted in the film reacquaints franchise fans with the lure of an ancient puzzle box—as well as the consequences of temptation. A businessman named Roland Voight (Goran Višnjić) tricks a sex worker into becoming his latest sacrifice.

Fast forward six years. Trevor persuades Riley to help him break into a warehouse to access an abandoned shipping container. Inside, they find only the ancient puzzle box. Though unaware of its purpose, Riley quickly becomes obsessed with it.

Following a fight, Riley's brother kicks her out of the apartment in the middle of the night. She wanders around the neighborhood, stopping first at her car where she finds pills and takes them. She ends up sitting on a merry-go-round in a public park, fidgeting with the box until she accidentally solves it—though she avoids getting cut by one of its blades.

Having been summoned, the Cenobites—a group of sadistic beings from another dimension—arrive on the scene and insist that she must choose another as a sacrifice. Unfortunately, Matt shows up at the worst possible moment.

Knowing she is at fault for Matt's fate, Riley is determined to save him. In doing so, she learns the secrets of the puzzle box and inadvertently puts those around her in grave danger. The trail eventually leads her to a creepy estate in the woods once owned by Voight but abandoned after his disappearance and presumed death.

Jamie Clayton portrays the Priest, leader of the Cenobites, modeled after the franchise icon, Pinhead. Her take on the sadistic character is as sinister as it is sensual. She is simultaneously terrifying and angelic, and she brings a hypnotic authority to the role that illustrates how an entity so inhospitable can be equally irresistible.

The congregation of loyal Cenobites features marvelously ghastly designs, as if fashion in their plane of existence is preoccupied by stylish gore and chic mutilation. There are callbacks to Cenobites from previous films, such as the Chatterer, played here by Jason Liles.

Gasp, played by Selina Lo, is of particular note due both to the character's exquisite creepiness as well as the fact that she—unlike most of the Priest's subordinates—has a few lines of dialog. Other Cenobites showcased in the film include the Weeper (Yinka Olorunnife), the Asphyx (Zachary Hing), the Masque (Vukasin Jovanovic), and the Mother (Gorica Regodic).

The writing is solid, though at times derivative. Ben Collins and Luke Piotrowski deliver a refreshing take that works as a metaphor for the consequences of selfishness and making bad life choices.

Riley's addiction and her unwillingness to take responsibility for her life impacts the lives of those around her. Her psychological urges toward self-destruction have real world consequences for her family and friends. Unfortunately, this causes the plot to sometimes slouch into slasher-film mode as characters are picked off one by one.

Unlike Ashley Laurence's squeaky clean central character in the original film, Riley is fraught with flaws that initially make her quite unlikable. Her journey of transformation is both powerful and tragic.

The film emphasizes religious implications without endorsing the idea that the Cenobites are anything more than inter-dimensional entities. The viewer can ascribe supernatural meaning should they choose to do so.

The fact that the story explores the idolization of pain and suffering as a fetish certainly suggests it can be viewed as an allegory for religious masochism. One can't help but liken traveling flagellants of the Middle Ages to Barker's Cenobites.

Bruckner's *Hellraiser* also suffers from pacing issues. The first act is slow and lumbering.

Let's be honest: Everyone came for the Cenobites, and the story forces the viewer to wade through a lot of drawn-out tableaus establishing personalities and relationships before there is any substantial revelation. Building up tension is fine, but it's nice to get an early indication how scary—and bloody—things are likely to get for our hapless soon-to-be victims.

Hellraiser is not a remake, though it borrows elements from the first two films in the franchise: *Hellraiser* in 1987 and *Hellbound: Hellraiser II* in 1988. It's better than *Hellbound*, but not as good as the original.

It does serve to reenergize the 35-year-old franchise and expand the mythology of the Cenobites. In Riley, the film gives viewers a more fully developed character whose past mistakes and continuing struggles highlight both her vulnerability and her grit. It is fittingly gruesome, ambitious, and morbidly fascinating.

Though it may not tear your soul apart, it certainly has some grisly sights to show you.

Lee Clark Zumpe is entertainment editor at Tampa Bay Newspapers, a Tomatometer-Approved Critic, and an author of short fiction appearing in select anthologies and magazines. Follow Lee at www.patreon.com/Haunter_of_the_Bijou.

Late Night with the Devil
Review by Lee Clark Zumpe

Solid performances, clever premise save "Late Night with the Devil."

Before diving into the new supernatural horror film *Late Night with the Devil*, let's reflect upon a decade of high strangeness. Everything seemed much scarier in the 1970s. Not just horror movies: I mean reality itself seemed to be tinged with dread and lurking fear.

The late 1960s hippie movement brought the concept of the Age of Aquarius to Middle America and somehow spawned a resurgence of interest in parapsychological phenomena such as telepathy, clairvoyance and psychokinesis. This trend wasn't confined to fringe religious groups.

In 1970, *McCall's* — a popular monthly American women's magazine that had a long history of avoiding any subject matter that could be considered provocative or controversial — dedicated practically an entire issue to "the occult explosion," covering topics like astrology, magic, tarot, Satan worship, and seances. The lead article claimed that astrology had "taken the place of psychology as the personality decoder" of the younger generation.

Many other 1970s mainstream publications covered the topic. *Time* printed stories such as "Astrology and the New Cult of the Occult" and "The Occult Revival: Satan Returns." *Newsweek* published "The Cult of the Occult." *Look* added to the mix with "Witchcraft is Rising." Maybe it's because I was still a kid, but it seemed like every house in the neighborhood might be haunted, and that every wooded lot in the area might be visited by witches performing rituals.

This preoccupation with the paranormal filtered its way down to kids, too: In elementary school, I remember reading *The Golden Book of the Mysterious*, published in 1976, which covered everything from witchcraft and fortunetelling to ghosts and werewolves.

Talk shows and reality television series hopped onto the bandwagon in the 1970s. Alan Landsburg produced "In Search of...," a series devoted to mysterious phenomena, hosted by Leonard Nimoy. The show originally ran from 1977 to 1982. Alan Landsburg Productions also developed *That's Incredible,* which presented a wide mix of stunts and exceptional people along with reenactments of purportedly paranormal events.

That's the contextual backdrop for *Late Night with the Devil*. Written, directed, and edited by Colin and Cameron Cairnes, the film blends the found-footage format with mockumentary filmmaking. It was released in theaters on March 22, 2024, by IFC Films. It became available for streaming on Shudder on April 19.

The conceit is that the shocking master tape of a long-lost live broadcast from Halloween night, 1977, has been uncovered. It is the final episode of a late-night talk show called *Night Owls*. Its host, Jack Delroy (David Dastmalchian), is in the midst of a savage ratings battle with rival Johnny Carson of *The Tonight Show*.

Hoping to stage a ratings coup, Delroy and Leo Fiske (Josh Quong Tart), the show's producer, have scheduled guests for a special occult-themed episode. Among those appearing are Christou (Fayssal Bazzi), a psychic; Carmichael Haig (Ian Bliss), a former magician turned skeptic; June Ross-Mitchell (Laura Gordon), a parapsychologist and author; and a teen named Lilly (Ingrid Torelli), the survivor of a mass suicide at a Satanic church. June, who acts as Lilly's guardian, believes the girl suffers from a "psychic infestation," which is a pseudoscientific euphemism for being possessed by a demon.

After a documentary-style introduction laying the groundwork, *Late Night with the Devil* plunges into the found-footage portion of the film. Initially, it's slow going. An awkward opening monologue is followed by the inevitable clumsy banter with Jack's comedic sidekick, Gus McConnell (Rhys Auteri).

The filmmakers maintain a low boil through the most of Christou's act, as he delivers hit-or-miss cold readings for audience members. Then the psychic gets an unexpected premonition, falls ill, spews a stream of black vomit, is carried off stage by his handler and dies on the way to the hospital. So much for Christou.

This is the filmmakers turning on the "fasten your seatbelts" sign.

Except, the pace slows down again. In addition to presenting the raw master tape, and in keeping with the subjective documentary format, "never-before-seen" behind-the-scenes footage of the evening's taping fill in the gaps between the broadcast segments. Viewers get to see the growing concern of crewmembers as high strangeness pervades the set. We get to see heated exchanges between Jack and Gus. We get to see evidence of an inappropriate relationship between Jack and June.

Aside from poor Christou's demise, it takes about an hour to get to the meat of the matter. Jack basically bullies a reluctant June into conjuring up Abraxas, Lilly's demon. This was, of course, his objective all along.

As it turns out, it was also the demon's goal.

I won't reveal exactly how this on-air invocation descends into pandemonium, or the associated details of Jack's private life and the Faustian bargain he made which all contribute to the climax. The movie mostly goes where one expects it to go, with a few surprising detours along the way.

The filmmakers did a fantastic job setting the scene with spot-on set and costume design and ample pop culture references, ranging from Jimmy Carter jokes to lowbrow sketch comedy bits that served as late-night entertainment in the 1970s. There are veiled allusions to psychic spoon-bender Uri Geller, magician-turned-skeptic James Randi, Church of Satan founder Anton Szandor LaVey, and the Amazing Kreskin. The script even dances around the secretive Bohemian Grove cabal. Likewise, there are references to 1970s horror touchstones: Gus, for instance, whips out a department store cross necklace and starts chanting "the power of Christ compels you" like Max von Sydow playing Father Merrin in "The Exorcist."

Does it all work? In my opinion: barely. The creative premise alone is enough to give *Late Night with the Devil* a passing grade, although I don't feel the need to add any gold stars or happy faces. It lacks cohesiveness. Its tone vacillates between black comedy and horror—and yet its campiest aspects failed to make me laugh and its scariest bits didn't elicit a single flinch.

The conclusion, in particular, was profoundly disappointing and completely undermined the setup. In retrospect, a handful of performances saved this film from being a complete fiasco. Dastmalchian does an excellent job of playing the fame-hungry celebrity willing to do anything to score a ratings win. When the script allows it, Torelli is uber-creepy. The clips of Lilly staring directly into the camera looking unhinged are far more effective than anything shown in the possession sequence. Other standouts include Gordon and Tart, each of whom totally inhabit their characters. On the other hand, I think Steve Mouzakis, who portrays Szandor D'Abo, may have studied Tom Neyman's performance as *The Master in Manos: The Hands of Fate* to prepare for his role.

Of course, one must consider how difficult it must be to act like you aren't acting—to make the events that are supposedly happening in real time feel authentic, even though each scene is rehearsed and reshot multiple times.

As a viewer, I felt like the filmmakers had difficulty settling on the film's prevailing tenor. They sadly failed to achieve a unity of effect. Once you embrace the film's erratic nature, it becomes more palatable. For all the effort and imagination that went into making *Late Night with the Devil*, it's worth a watch.

Lee Clark Zumpe is entertainment editor at Tampa Bay Newspapers, a Tomatometer-Approved Critic, and an author of short fiction appearing in select anthologies and magazines. Follow Lee at www.patreon.com/Haunter_of_the_Bijou.

The Crawling Chaos by Lee Clark Zumpe

The Crawling Chaos, like a plague of grief
Swept over the globe to our disbelief,
Defiling our souls, infecting our blood,
A torrent of pain, we fell to the flood.

At first, he contrived to twist all our fears:
A blight of mistrust strung out over years;
Then he who craves death, Haunter of the Dark,
Set fire to this world with one timely spark:

His virus spread wide, leveling empires,
Our loved ones we sent to funeral pyres.
Survivors, we few, watch darkness descend,
Across this cold earth as we near the end.

Now after the storm, no hope remaining,
Anarchy spreading, charity waning,
I offer my soul where my body falls;
And now I must go: Nyarlathotep calls.

Crime Scene Confidential
by
Marc Shapiro

Hardcase had seen it all. Which was why they called him Hardcase.

Burned beyond recognition. Decapitations. Slasher victims. Mass shooting victims in which body parts were scattered for days. He had the stomach for it. He barely twitched at the sickest and vile examples of man's inhumanity to man. He was the go-to investigator when a 911 resulted in more blood and guts than ten mortals could tolerate without tossing their cookies.

Calls to Hardcase invariably came between midnight and 3:00 a.m., when bloodlust and horrendous acts were abroad in the land. And it was usually his understanding wife Nancy, aroused from a good night's sleep, who said nothing but groggily handed the phone to her husband. Hardcase, equally full of slumber, listened as the Watch Commander mumbled a garble of info. He clicked off the phone and got dressed. Nancy had been around this scenario endless times and responded with her own marching orders...

"Don't forget to shower when you get home. And no good morning wake-up kisses until I know where you've been."

Hardcase mumbled an "I love you too" and was out the door and into the night.

The location was a flop house/slaughterhouse on the wrong side of town. No life worth much would have or could have lived there. But as he surveyed the flea-infested rooms and took sketchy notes in an old school notebook, Hardcase reasoned that no life worth living here should have died this way.

Even by his standards, this was a grotesque mess on steroids. A butcher shop of head, hands, arms, legs, and torsos everywhere he looked. And his keen sense of the crime scene was quick to pick up on the fact that there was no blood anywhere.

A bloodcurdling scream shot through the room from the hallway. The landlady who called this mess in hadn't stopped screaming for hours. And who could blame her? It was that damnable smell of death that had driven her to hysterics. She had opened the door on the crime scene and was immediately driven to madness.

Hardcase stepped out of the room as the blood boys bagged the remains and took them away. He jotted down a few more notes for his report. He smiled a tight, rueful smile. He knew how this would play out. He knew what would happen next. It would be yet another one of his reports filed away and forgotten. Because nobody wanted to get within spitting distance of another of his wacky crime scene reports.

But Hardcase knew the facts. The perps were vampires, most likely more than one. It was strictly amateur hour. Pros take the blood and run. Amateurs like to leave a mess.

The End

Forever After by Marc Shapiro

She was psychologically damaged and scarred
He was sad, alone and forever melancholy
How they met and fell in love was anybody's guess
To their respective circles
it wasn't so much a dream come true
As it was a nightmare
But here they were
Alone in their pain and isolation
All these years later
Together
They had very little in common
Except that they were both night people
Who preferred to do their hunting alone

Tongue Vampire by Denny E. Marshall

Vampire hunter
Examines recent victim
Body drained of blood
Yet no double puncture wounds
Visible on neck

Alien bloodsucker has no fangs
Its tongue stretches at will
Transforms into cylinder shape
Inserts long tube down victims' mouth
Until it reaches the heart
Takes less then a minute
To empty entire contains

A female slayer discovers new breed
With her powers able to pull away
From his lips before loss to great
Wooden spike effective on celestial
She reports finding to colleagues

Haiku by Denny E. Marshall

chose not to dump you
she changes places with twin
vampire sister

Words in the Waiting House
by
Todd Hanks

Narrator: The wind tore at the shutters as if it had claws, and the house waited. The house had waited since it was created. Or, to be exact, it had waited off and on. Between the times unfortunate people had chosen to move in. Lightening made streaks across the ebony sky. Inside, a chandelier and a fireplace poker discussed Beethoven. The rafters and the wood floor sang old folk ditties. Then a spoon spoke.

Spoon: You know, Spool, I was a beautiful woman once. Before the devil changed me to a spoon.

Spool: I don't believe a word of it.

Spoon: I swear, Spool, by my sterling silver heart every word I speak is true.

Spool: Never did believe a word you ever say, Spoon. Not a word. Wouldn't you agree, Fire Bellows?

Fire Bellows: Yes, Spool. All spoons are pathological liars.

Spoon: I resent that. I had blonde hair and green eyes. I had a favorite dress. I was a princess, too. The devil fell in love with me, tried to seduce me. But I wasn't having any of that. I was a good girl. So spurned, Satan turned and changed me into the utensil you see before you.

Fire Bellows: Why do you sound like a man, then?

Spoon: The voice came with the spoon shape.

Spool: Lie, lie, lie.

Spoon: My original voice was as effeminate as a daisy chain and as clear as birdsong. Sweet and golden, like honey made from godlike bees.

Fire Bellows: You're as cracked as a flowerpot.

Spoon: But that's not the whole story. Every year, the devil comes to me and changes me back into my human form just long enough to ask me again to marry him. But I have my honor, and every year I choose to remain in the form of a spoon.

Spool: Nutty as a tree.

Spoon: Sometimes he takes me into the Underworld before changing me back to being a spoon.

Fire Bellows: My, my. He takes you into the Underworld, does he?

Spoon: Sometimes.

Spool: So, Spoon. I've always wondered. Just what does the Underworld look like? I'm sure you can make up something vivid.

Fire Bellows: Yes. What indeed does the Underworld look like? I imagine it's a hell of a sight!

Spoon: It isn't like the inside of a cave. There is a sky and mountains and lakes, rivers of orange lava. There are dinosaurs swimming in the steaming water, with long curved green necks and teeth like spear points. There are giants and tribes of purple pygmies. There are gods and mythological monsters of ancient Greece of carved ivy on time-cracked white columns.

Spool: You're what's time-cracked.

Narrator: The air in the Waiting House grew uncomfortably warm. The walls bled. Steam rose from the couch and armchairs. A boar's head with tusks on the wall twisted and turned, its tongue rolling out its mouth and back and forth. And suddenly, Satan appeared in the middle of the living room. He wore a long, red cloak. His head was a bare skull with snakes for hair. The vipers curled from the hood. His voice bellowed as he spoke to the spoon.

Satan: Once again, I stand before you. Do you not fear me? I could make things much worse for you.

Spoon: Why would I fear you? You've already turned me into a spoon. How's it going to get worse for me?

Satan: I could turn you into a fork!

Spoon: Oh, how lucky I'd feel being a fork. Nothing I'd enjoy more. Things would just run through me, instead of me having to hold them. Oh, to be a fork.

Satan: Well, I could melt you in a fiery furnace!

Spoon: That sounds so warm. Toasty warm. It gets so cold here in the evening. Oh, how I'd love to be melted down in a furnace.

Satan: You have an annoying personality. But, the more you push me away, the more I want you. Well anyway, you know why I came here. You know what I'm going to ask you. First, I will turn you into a young woman again.

Narrator: Blue, shimmering lines of neon light emitted from the spoon, and then the utensil changed into a green-eyed, blonde young lady in a white gown. Now, her voice was delicate and effeminate.

Fire Bellows: I'll be damned.

Spoon: You said you had something to ask me.

Satan: You know I do.

Spoon: But you don't ask, do you?

Satan: What do you mean?

Spoon: You demand. You tell me I have to marry you. There's no romance there. You're a control freak.

Satan: I never thought of the situation like that. I have to admit I'm used to being in charge.

Spoon: You've never even asked me if I'm attracted to you.

Satan: Are you attracted to me?

Spoon: I could get used to the skull head with snakes. You'd make a good tattoo. But you have to learn to treat a lover with respect. Drop the monster thing and be a gentleman.

Satan: Well, I am the king of evil and all.

Spoon: I'm talking about your private life. Your family life. The chaos of devastation you create, stealing souls and all, torturing sinners, I'm not saying don't do it. But leave it at work. When you get home, be a gentleman. Warm up my towel in the dryer while I shower. Have flowers delivered to me. Use your imagination. Wacky, romantic stuff.

Satan: Wacky, romantic stuff, eh? Ah hell. Okay. I'll give it a go. Madam, may I escort you to the underworld?

Spoon: Now you're talking.

The End

Flight of the Barons by Matthew Wilson

Before the sunrise the barons fled
Those creatures loyal to the count
Using the terror of his name for their greed
To safeguard their castles of bloodstone.

Human survivors pushed those foundations to the sea
Burning their torn flags of war
The slowest runaways were butchered
Staked by silver on the hangman's crossroad.

The barons were good men long ago
Before the count turned them to his puppets
He knocked them from their lofty pedestals
To personal executioners of his whims.

The resistance poisoned their feasts with no effect
Before they collected into a peasant's revolt
Hanging the eldest baron from the spire
Sending out a loud message to his allies.

Now before the sunrise the barons fled
Back to their master who despises failure
Feeding his useless puppets to his children
Bulking them up to take on the hope of resistance.

His war horns blast snow from the mountains
Waking fanged beasts that won him his throne
While the last living waits nervous on the battlefield
To send this monsters family back to hell.

The Forests of Katla
by
Lee Clark Zumpe

This place is nothing like home.

From dusk till the first fiery traces of dawn, more than 150 earth hours pass. Imagine, if you can, a night that lasts a full earth week. I find myself yearning for the gentle touch of crimson light from an alien star.

I am alone on my patrol tonight.

The territory to which my company has been assigned does not have an equal upon the earth of the 24th century. The vast shadow-haunted forests that blanketed much of Europe in the distant past could serve as an adequate reference. But, there are things here that have never been on Earth. In these darkened woods, nature has been given the freedom to explore its savage bounds to excess.

There are blackened pools of stagnant water from which man-sized frog-like things pollute the night air with their hideous songs. Winged serpents perch upon the limbs of trees, their yellow eyes aglow in the gloom. I have seen plants pull their roots up from the soil and shamble off in search of a meal.

It is no wonder that the first colony that tried to tame this land was instead consumed by it.

A cold wisp of air carries upon it the scent of the enemy. Quickly, I focus my senses and calculate the distance. Instinct tells me they are few in number – I could carry out the attack alone, but that is not our way.

I mark the location and swiftly return to my company.

We were all so naive.

We led comfortable lives on Earth. Most of us left behind families—wives and children we will never see again. Earth, for all its flaws, was paradise compared to this. We have forsaken the comforts of technology, security, and relationships.

And for what?

So that humankind can one day build permanent settlements here? So that a new civilization can be forged? So that another world's resources can be depleted?

Everything is done for the sake of the empire, no matter how antiquated the term may be.

My commander calls the other scouts back to the base camp. Wordlessly, she develops a plan of attack. She is a firm believer in the use of overwhelming force.

Two hundred men and women make up our company. Ages range from 17 to 63. Among us are representatives from every race and every major religion. Ours is one of several dozen such companies that were placed on this planet to eradicate the dominant life forms.

We are not the first attempt at pest control here.

Seventy-two years ago, a fleet of ships arrived in orbit around the planet we call Katla. Two hundred thousand well-trained soldiers carrying hi-tech weapons landed on the surface.

They erected a camp and secured it. They set up a communications network. They planted crops to supply food in the coming years. And when they were ready, they marched out into the forest and began their conquest.

Within a month, not one soldier remained. Many were killed in night-time skirmishes and raids. Some went into the bush and simply disappeared. The bulk of the invasion force, however, died in a bloody battle along a ravine. Their bones are still there—I've seen them.

Back on Earth, the battle was referred to as the Red River Massacre. The details were deemed too horrible to report to the masses.

Back on Earth, the popular belief is that we are in contention with an alien race that possesses technology comparable to our own. In fact, the enemy has yet to develop the wheel, let alone matter/anti-matter repulsar weaponry. The fact that the military cannot conquer Katla is a considerable embarrassment that could destroy careers and even topple governments.

And so, when their technology proved ineffective, they tapped us.

After centuries of fear, persecution, intolerance, and denial, they came to us with a proposition.

We are moving rapidly now, each of us keenly aware of everyone else's position. Unlike our poor, bumbling predecessors, we employ the dark forest of Katla as an ally. We immerse ourselves in the folds of her green flesh and cover ourselves with the cloak of her night. Long before we see the enemy, we can smell their putrid odor on the breeze.

It is fortunate I did not attack them alone.

Many more of them have gathered. It might be that they are planning a counter-strike against us. The threat of our presence in their world has caused them to evolve. They are forming well-structured clans to defend their homes. They are sharpening bones to use as daggers. They have developed tactics, and they practice for battle.

Tonight, however, it is clear that they are unaware of our approach. In a few moments, we will pounce upon them from the tangled thickets and shadowy brush.

Even now, as my heart pounds and the blood rushes through my veins, I still wonder if we made the right decision. We only agreed to their terms so that those of us who stayed behind would never again know the fear of our ancestors. The burden of our existence has been lifted, and the global community has embraced us.

Little good that does us here, so far from Earth.

The commander gives the signal, and we charge. Our bloodthirsty howls drown out the screams of the enemy. Terrified, they scatter as 200 werewolves fall upon them in the strange forests of Katla.

The End

Get Of Dragon by Kendall Evans

The giant net, immense
Twelve years in the weaving
Is designed to capture dragons
Rockets derived from fireworks
Are attached along one side

To loft the net into the sky
For the Kingdom of Grimoire
Is constantly threatened by dragons
Who nest in the surrounding mountains
And lakes and caves—

River dragons, too, abound—
And there is a strange legend
Here in the Kingdom of Grimoire
That tells of a hero, a dragon slayer
Who will one day be dragon-born

Not surprising, for a populace
Always in danger of losing
Their lives, their children,
Their livestock to dragons—
To invent such a tall tale

And believe in it, wholeheartedly—
Not long after the making of the net
A dragon attacked from the sky—
All was in preparation, however
The rockets all firing in unison

The giant net launched upward
Up and over the descending dragon—
All encumbered in tangles of net
The dragon known as Garthon
Fell helplessly from the sky

Snoke and flames spouting
From outsized nostrils
From the dragon's cavernous maw
As Garthon spectacularly crash-landed
Atop the castle's watchtower

Sprawling over mortared crenelations
And vomiting forth the corpse
Of a child recently consumed—
And then the dying dragon
Plummeted from the ramparts

Onto the hard cobblestones far below—
"And yet, and yet
She is not quite dead yet"
The kingdom's sorceress declared
"Though her heart beats so faintly

Though her breaths are so shallow
I will save the life of this child
And nurse her back to health."—
Only the formidable sorceress Gwiydolyn
Believed this a possibility

Given the state of the child.
The girl's lips moved and muttered
From the depths of a comatose dream—
Her flesh scalded raw-red
Her hair eaten away

By acidic digestive fluids—
And from thence she was carried
To the bed of a deceased
Princess of Grimoire
Who had died in the jaws of a dragon

Where the sorceress slowly
Coaxed the child back to life
And consciousness, a miracle
Akin to resurrecting the dead—
Months later, the child awakened

Her tender young flesh badly burned
And marred by scars all over
Her scalded lungs laboring
Like noisy leather bellows
As she breathed, out and in—

Sprouts of hair eventually appeared
Upon her naked scalp—
As her hair grew slowly back in
n disobedient thatches and patches
Always to be unruly, as was she

She was perhaps a mere eight-years-old
When she was born forth in dragon spew—
By the time she was twelve
She had for the most part healed—
Though scarred, was she, from head to toe

She practiced most rigorously
From dawn to the depths of the night
Learning weaponry, and soldiering
Declaring and swearing all dragons
To be her mortal enemies

She honed her skills
With spears and swords
Always five knives and more
Concealed about her person—
She was forever marred, was she

With whorls of scars
And puckered flesh
Cicatrices scaling her skin
Blue-purpled in sundry places—
Scalp still bare here and there—

By her twelfth birthday
Her age estimated
She resembled a skinny boy warrior
Agile and muscular, fierce-eyed,
Intent, strong of will, dedicated—

And yet, she was so very beautiful—
Here mere presence captured all eyes
And the King's Soldiers whispered sly innuendoes—
And this small-breasted, comely body
Of hers, her stance always so heroic—

And so, upon that fateful day
Arbitrarily deemed her twelfth birthday
The sorceress Gwyndolyn called a meeting
Gathering all of the clans of Grimoire together
In the great hall of the castle:

"We all know all too well
The legend of a child born unto a dragon—
She before us is that legend,
That legacy; She fulfills the prophecy
She will be our salvation, our dragon slayer—

It is her heritage; her destiny—"
Declared by the sorceress Gwyndolyn
In her practiced Celtic eloquence—
"I have thus named her and now I proclaim her
Mionlaigh Dragan, slayer of dragons—"

Eel Soup
by
Marge Simon

So, the time has come. He can't stand watching her suffer any longer.

He prepares their last meal from scratch. He has procured the vegetables from the neighbor's garden. The onions are still good, as well as the carrots and potatoes. A can of stewed tomatoes, peppercorns and salt—these are in the cabinet. The most important ingredient of all—the eels, he has obtained at the docks early this morning. He is careful to add them with their blood as the soup cools. They are finely chopped and raw, camouflaged with cabbage leaves. A modified and deadly vichyssoise served in her shining silver tureen.

He wheels her chair to the table. She's so frail now, her skin almost transparent. The plague that sweeps the world hasn't touched him as yet. Perhaps he is one of the few who is resistant. He frowns at the irony. His own life isn't worth bothering with – but hers is another story. Such talents she has, so much to look forward to! Her paintings were selling well. She had begun composing music to accompany the presentations in galleries. She called it "bonding kinetic transitions." But no more—this strain of the virus knows no prejudice.

He picks up a photograph of them when they were young, remembers the smell of her wool coat, the way her mouth chokes back a laugh in the photo. She'd loved his jokes – even the lame ones. Then came a time when laughter stopped. Like the sound of her voice, a bare whisper now.

Once, she'd said his dreams were all smashed up inside. "Gray on gray. Form without substance," she said. She was the artist. She had dreams for both of them. They are silent during dinner. He offers her another helping. To his surprise, she nods with a lopsided smile. *She knows.* He turns away to wipe his eyes. After dinner, he helps her out of the wheelchair, lays her gently on the bed. The muscle cramping will begin soon, ending the beating of her heart.

But instead of closing her eyes and lying back, she pushes herself up. "Hand me that novel you were reading to me last night, sweetheart. I am feeling so much better; I should like to find out how it ends myself." He is stunned. This is the first time she's said entire sentences in many days. And wanting to read? How can this be—the eels have cured the virus? Her eyes are bright and her pulse steady. There's a healthy flush to her cheeks that wasn't there before dinner.

As he hands her the book, he feels a sharp pain in his stomach as the cramps begin. With a terrible chill, he remembers it was to be *their* last meal.

The End

Interview with a Reluctant Vampire
by
Margaret L. Carter

Silhouetted against the full moon, a bat flapped outside the closed bedroom window. Before Marie's eyes, it dissolved into mist and oozed through the minute crack between the frame and the sill. Motionless on her bed, through slitted lids, she watched the mist coalesce into a dark-haired, slender, young-looking man.

As he loomed over her, she thrust a silver cross on a chain around her neck into his face. He recoiled, hissing.

"How about that, I guessed right—you really are a vampire!" She couldn't suppress the delight in her voice.

While he stood frozen in shock at her odd reaction, she sprang out of bed, dashed to the window, and hung a rosary from the latch to drape over the lower pane.

Whirling around, he snarled at seeing his escape blocked.

"Don't try to leave yet." Marie plumped the pillows to lean against as she sat on the bed. After switching on the nightstand lamp, she donned her wire-rimmed bifocals and picked up a notepad and pen. "I have a ton of questions."

He bared his teeth. "Foolish woman, why aren't you afraid? I'm here to drink your blood."

"Which you've already done at least three times." She rubbed the tiny scabs on her throat. "You must not drain much at once, because I'm still in decent health. Wow, you have fangs just like in the movies." No cape, though. He wore a black shirt and tight, black jeans. So he didn't embrace popular culture cliches.

"Movies, bah!"

"Don't hover like that. This could take a while." She gestured toward the desk chair, and he grudgingly sat down. "As I said, I want to ask you some questions."

"Why should I answer them? And how did you realize you were a vampire's victim in this scientific age?" He spoke with a hint of a Spanish accent.

"I'm an anthropology professor. I teach a class in legends and superstitions, and I plan to include a unit on vampire lore."

"You would expose me?" he growled.

Marie shook her head. "I'll attribute anything you say to an anonymous informant." She poised the pen over the notepad. "It's the least you can do after stealing my blood."

"Stealing? I take only what I need."

"Do you need blood to survive? Would you die without it? And would animal blood work as well as human?"

"Yes, not exactly—fall into a state of suspended animation—and no. Animal blood serves in emergencies, but only as a stopgap."

"Now, how many ounces do you drink per feeding?"

"How should I know? I don't measure it." He glanced at the window.

"You might as well cooperate. The sooner we finish the interview, the sooner I remove the rosary. The door's protected, too, by the way. Do all holy symbols repel you or only crosses?"

"That depends on the individual vampire's background and beliefs. I was a Catholic in life."

She jotted notes as he answered. "Do you sleep by day in a coffin lined with your native soil? And does sunlight kill you?"

He rubbed his forehead as if it pained him. "Please, one question at a time, woman. The sun only weakens us. As for native earth, I'm on it at all times. I've dwelt here since Spain ruled this land. And no need to lie in a coffin. That's movie nonsense."

"Can you change into other shapes besides bat and mist? How about a wolf? Does garlic affect you? Silver? Can you consume food or liquids other than blood?" She brightened up as a lesser known superstition occurred to her. "Do you have a compulsion to count small objects like grains or pebbles? If so, I could've saved myself some trouble and just trapped you by scattering rice on the floor."

"Enough!" he roared, covering his ears.

"Come on, you owe me. What about your other powers? Do you have the strength of twenty men? If I weren't wearing this cross, could you control my mind? How did you become a vampire? How does the transformation work? Does it hurt? How can a vampire be destroyed? Not that I would try."

"No more questions! Let me out of this blasted room, and I swear I'll never come near you again."

"You promise?"

"My word of honor as a hidalgo. I'd rather be staked out under the desert sun at high noon than endure another minute of your blathering."

Marie strode across the room, removed the cross, and opened the window. The vampire leaped into the air, transforming into a bat in the process, and soared into the night.

"Well, that clears up one issue—the pen is mightier than the stake."

The End

We, the Possessed
by
Rajeev Bhargava

"Help!"

Something evil had been unleashed as a frightened, frail figure in a tattered dress ran barefoot for her life through dense forestry from an invisible entity coming fast towards her in broad daylight.

Every time she glanced back, she saw trees being uprooted and crashing to the ground as it advanced closer, toying with its prey, enjoying her anguish and suffering before thrusting her onto the ground. She tried to get up but found herself being controlled. Blood dripped from her nostrils, and her eyes rolled over yellow, protruding from their sockets. After that, her mouth opened wide, and there followed a piercing scream so loud that it echoed in the air.

She then heard a pained moan as the entity entered her body, after which "she" rose to her feet and made "her" way out of the forest towards the city.

The Previous Day: In their 66-storey New York apartment on the top floor of the sky-scraper, a family consisting of two sisters with three children—two girls and a boy belonging to the older sister—emerged from the lift and entered their New York apartment.

Later that evening, after unpacking, the two sisters laid out the table.

"Elaine, Peter, Angela, I won't say it a second time; dinner is served, so turn down the music and join us at the table ... now!"

Beth smiled at her older sister, placing a napkin across her neck. "You really love to pamper them, Big Sis."

Angelina's eyes widened. "Look who's talking," she replied, gazing at the gifts Beth had placed in her handbag.

"Coming, Mom!" replied Selena, the youngest sibling who had just turned nine. She entered the kitchen, holding a rag doll with pins through it. With headphones on, Cathy, 13, and Robbie, 15, followed.

No sooner had they sat down to enjoy their meal than everything around them shook from under their feet. Some of the furniture fell and broke, as did cutlery and antiques.

"Earthquake," said Robbie.

After a few minutes, everything was still, and they sat and gazed at each other wide-eyed.

"Mom, can we go and buy a large pizza and a coke?" asked Selena, the spoilt baby of the house.

****

Outside, a wide crack had formed in the surrounding car park, and Robbie was the first to see it.

As he approached, he knelt down and, to his surprise, saw a large basement. It was pitch-black below, so he lit his pen torch and turned to his sisters.

"Hey! There's a basement below. I'm going down to take a closer look. I won't be long, I promise."

"Fine, but don't take long," said Cathy.

"Please do!" said Selena. "While we enjoy your share of pizza with coke."

Just then, a decomposed hand reached out and ripped its talons into his legs, then dragged him down into the darkness.

"Robbie!" they called out, alarmed.

He screamed.

"What do we do now, Cathy?" asked Selena, giving her sister a tight hug. "Did you see what I saw?"

Cathy nodded, caressing Selena's hair.

"It all happened so fast, but it looked like something gruesome grabbed Robbie's leg and dragged him down below."

"Oh, you poor soul," said Cathy. "You're only nine and having to go through all this. I should drop you back at the flat, and then we can tell Mom all about it.

"But Selena, Mom will be mad at us."

****

At their hotel apartment, Angelina wore a stern look, which she would give to her children, who were still not back. She found herself fidgeting and biting her nails.

"Beth, the earthquake seems to have subsided. Could you go down and find out where they are?" asked Angelina

"Oh, okay."

No sooner had Beth said those words when they heard the main corridor lift bell sound and the doors slid open. Cathy ran forwards and gave her mother a tight hug. Angelina caressed her and stared at Selena.

"Where's Robbie?"

The girls gazed at each other and then back at their mother.

Angelina stormed in their direction and past them, pressing the lift button. As she entered to go down, she called out to Beth, "Make sure they don't get up to any more mischief. I'll be back with Robbie, no matter how late it gets. If you need to rest, please do so. Don't wait up for me."

Beth nodded and called out, "Oh, sis! Be careful of weirdoes. It's Halloween in ten minutes!" She glanced at her watch.

The lift doors closed, and the girls returned to the flat at the sound of thunder. As the lift began its journey to the basement, there was another tremor, and everything around Angelina shook; then, the lights went out, and the lift froze.

Angelina looked around, infuriated.

****

Inside the cracked opening, Robbie, or what remained of him, stood like a wax doll, staring at a wrapped object wedged into a concrete wall. Around it were sinister drawings depicting witchcraft and human sacrificial rituals. He could only gaze at them, wide-eyed, but his will was being controlled by something evil that was using him as a tool to get that object out of the wall.

A feminine moan echoed; after that, Robbie felt an electric shock. Robbie's eyes fell on a table in the room, and on it was a pickaxe. He used it to crack open the wrapped object, which

72

he lifted off the ground. No sooner had he done so than he was supernaturally transported back into his bedroom. He snapped out of his trance.

Inside the lift, Angelina was livid and infuriated. She was a strong-willed and dedicated mother, but when the glow appeared out of thin air and engulfed her body, she felt a strange sensation. The same presence that had made its way through the forest just a few weeks ago had homed in and possessed her…

Just then, everything was back to normal, and the lift doors opened. Angelina stepped out barefoot and made her way to her apartment.

As Angelina entered, the apartment door was already open. It was dark inside, so when Beth, Cathy, and Selena noticed her from a distance, they ran towards her.

They landed in their mother's arms, and she wrapped her thin arms with yellow talons around their throats. After that, she came out into the light to face Beth.

Her eyeballs were yellow with red pupils. When Angelina opened her mouth, bloody drool fell to the floor. "Too bad, Beth," she said in a croaky voice. "It's just not your day, is it? Hah, ha, ha, ha, hah!"

Angelina looked at her, and Beth's body suddenly froze. She was paralysed. Then Angelina gazed into Selena and Cathy's eyes, hugged them tightly, and dissolved them into her womb. She then opened her mouth and puffed with all her force.

Slowly but surely, the apartment and the entire building evaporated and changed into a thick swampland. With an evil grin, Angelina made her way into quicksand, where she would rest the night. Then, in the morning, she'd wake up fresh and start looking for fresh victims on which to feast.

Tomorrow was going to be a busy day, full of fresh bloody kills…

To be continued…

Baalphegor, Demon of the Caves by Rajeev Bhargava

For those that have never come across me,
I am a demon of "discoveries," if you like,
And my disciples worship me in caves.
My open mouth is my "crevice" or "split"
Worshipped by the Moabites as Baalphegor of Mount Phegor;
I await innocent passersby,
To pounce on them and tear them limb to limb,
And hearing their pangs for help and release
While enjoying eating my victims ALIVE!!!

I Am Charlie Echo
by
Marc Shapiro

I am Charlie Echo.

I've been Charlie Echo since 1966. Since Vietnam. Since I was the last man out, the bombs bursting in air and bullshit patriotism, great Hendrix music. I had to call myself something, and Charlie Echo sounded cool.

Before I was Charlie Echo, I was who knows who?

A couple hundred years was a long time to remember who I had been before the bite; somewhere in the battle between the North and the South, someone set me up for eternity and a course filled with blood, night, and forever.

I am Charlie Echo who, when he was not living out immortality as a member of the undead, was always up for a good fight. If there was war or conflict, I was the first one in and the last one out. My mind had become damaged by my lot as a vampire. When I wasn't out in the night in the madness of a world at war, I quenched my thirst on blood, nightmares, bad dreams, and any number of flashbacks. Which were grist for my short stories, poetry and a growing reputation in the underground literary world. The money wasn't great, but when you are a prolific so-and-so, it all adds up.

Then, one day, I met a woman.

It didn't take long for her to figure me out. It was kind of kinky being with the dead and making love to somebody who had no pulse. She loved me. She tolerated the occasional war ventures, my nightly sojourns into the blood hunt, and the creative madness that paid the bills.

Because I loved her, I wanted to bite her so we could be together forever. But she was of the moment and immortality was not an option. And so, we lived a good life. Charlie Echo and his woman. I living forever. She aging with every year. Until the day she took sick and, some weeks later, she withered and died.

I was the closest thing to a vampire being in mourning for the better part of a year. Being alone with the sadness, the insanity, the churning into black, into the night, and, as always, the bite that sustained me in a different kind of hell.

I am Charlie Echo. Always on the prowl for the next woman who would get it, understand it, and offer love in exchange for immortality. If only she would take the bite.

Charlie Echo. Over and out.

The End

Where Men Had Seldom Trod
by
Lee Clark Zumpe

One: Frontier Massacre!

Colonel Benjamin Waddel:

It is with utmost earnestness that I appeal to your compassion and entreat your consideration in a matter of gravest concern amongst the loyal tenants of this province. A spate of aggression hitherto unseen in the westernmost hinterlands has resulted in the destruction or abandonment of several strategic outposts and considerable loss of life. Standing militias have been unsuccessful in quelling this vicious uprising and there is a growing belief that the violence may spread eastward toward the coast. As acting colonial governor, I humbly request your support in subduing this insurrection.

Zephaniah Pettyford
April, 1760

The mephitic putrescence corrupting the secluded cove confirmed their worst fears even before Elijah Greenheath and William Haley reached the remote site. An uncanny silence engulfed the steep-walled valley still thick with hemlock and poplar stands.

"This savagery is a grim omen considering the burden we bear," Greenheath said, inspecting the breadth of the butchery. On the face of it, the episode showed marked signs implicating the Cherokee; still, clouds of doubt had already formed in both men's minds. In a world riddled with enduring enigmas, the most plausible explanations often ceded to the extraordinary.

Greenheath knelt amidst a field of charred debris that had been the modest foothills settlement of Rowan. No stranger to the highlands, he had visited the outpost often during the decade since its founding and counted among its denizens more than one friend. News of its plunder traveled east along the Cherokee Path, obliging the travelers to make a portentous and unexpected detour.

No building had been spared the torch; no settler had been granted mercy. The dead lay where they had fallen, victims of a savage massacre. Their wounds varied in implementation but not in severity: Some had been shot while others had been butchered by tomahawk. Men, women and children had faced the same grim fate.

"Five or six days at most have passed since this took place. Much blood has been shed needlessly," said Haley, Greenheath's senior colleague. "The Cherokee are still on the warpath. I hesitate to think what has become of all the settlements and trading posts between Ninety-Six and Fort Prince George to the south." Once again, the uncomfortable peace between the colonists and the Cherokee had shattered, leaving a string of remote villages at increased risk. The presiding governor alleged French intrigue, but the catalyst behind the current hostilities more likely stemmed from an ill-fated Virginia expedition against the Ohio Shawnee in which a provincial regiment had abandoned their Cherokee allies without provisions. The regional magistrate, when reviewing legitimate grievances brought forward by the tribe's chief, yielded to ethnocentricity and refused to admit any misconduct in the matter. "Next," Haley continued, "the British will undoubtedly send troops into the Keowee valley in hopes of restoring order."

"The restoration of order would be better left to those who have grown accustomed to the ways of the Cherokee. If not for sporadic intervention by British authorities, provincial troops, and a handful of deceitful frontier administrators who today disregard the very treaties they forged yesterday, there would be no animosity, no distrust, and no need for war." Born to a patrician family, Greenheath had a far greater affinity for the pioneer than he had for the landed gentry. His father instilled in him admiration for the common man and deep-seated dissatisfaction with the haut monde. "The British, as you say, may dispatch a contingent of unqualified, ill-equipped regulars to protect their interests in the southern marches; but, I suspect, their continuing campaign against the French and their Algonquin and Huron supporters in the north will keep them from fielding any formidable force."

Though much inclined to forsake the trappings of his aristocratic heritage, Greenheath had availed himself of an education only ample wealth could guarantee. His parents had relocated from Staffordshire, England, to Charles Town, settling in coastal Smithville in the early 1720s. Fearing banishment due to his undiscovered but unflinching support of Francis Atterbury and his efforts to place James Francis Edward Stuart on the throne of England, his father left behind much of his fortune as well as the ancestral estate of West Wardour Abbey, not far from Shugborough Hall.

Greenheath's father recouped a great deal of his lost prosperity by establishing a trade and export business in struggling Smithville, a small seaport established not far from where the swarthy floods of the Kaldetseenee River empty into the Atlantic. The primary commodities channeled through his growing concern were peltries—mostly deerskins—for which there persisted a substantial European demand in the manufacture of breeches, gloves, and hats. While brother Ernest embraced the responsibilities of managing the enterprise upon their father's death, Elijah—eager to escape the insipid complacency of city life and explore the wilderness—traveled to the far ends of the frontier to meet with trappers, traders, colonists, and trailblazers, securing new contracts and solidifying old agreements.

Occasionally, inherited commitments compelled him into accepting supplementary chores.

For five years, he had crisscrossed the piedmont, surveyed the borderlands and traded with the inhabitants of the Overhill settlements strewn along the Unaka Mountains. In both the scattered colonial settlements and the remote Cherokee villages, Greenheath had become a familiar and welcome caller. His prowess as an established frontiersman had come to rival his skills as an executor and negotiator.

Likewise, he developed a capacity for handling covert operations for his late father's established English patrons—an avant-garde, orphic fraternity of academicians and literati known only as Sodalitas Invictus.

"Have you ever known such wanton savageness from your former Indian friends?" Haley nodded toward the corpse of a colonist, burned and ruthlessly mutilated. His face, limbs, and torso had been stripped bare of flesh, his eyes plucked from their sockets. His lower jaw dangled askew from the skull as if frozen in a final shriek of agony, the white of his teeth conspicuous against the crimson backdrop of exposed muscle. "Bearing in mind the information we are privy to in our current undertaking, I cannot help but wonder if the doom that came to

Rowan sprang from a more degenerate source than what we are prone to first imagine. What injustice could inspire such malice and malignity?"

"In all my years dealing with them, I have never known the Cherokee to be capable of such atrocities as this," Greenheath said, more closely inspecting the remains of the victims. Again and again, he found the bodies disfigured, dismembered, and defaced. The absence of animal tracks allowed him to eliminate the possibility of foraging scavengers affecting the gruesome wounds posthumously. A pattern of disproportionate injury materialized suggesting that the episode had been something more than a simple vengeful exploit or an aggressive act war. "These people suffered significant tortures before they were slain."

"Their anguish cannot be likened to any physical torment imaginable ..." An old man staggered from the underbrush, his tattered garments soiled with blood and mud. His own injuries, though less severe than those of his fellow villagers, would bring about his death in little time. A deep gash scored his right shoulder leaving a nub of protruding bone and a swathe of swollen, purple flesh. Horror, grief, and disbelief mingled in his vacant stare and bleak expression. "But for all the misery they endured, I mourn more for those the wicked ones spirited away."

"Sit and rest, good sir," Haley said, even as the colonist collapsed to the ground. Both men charged to his aid, together propping him against a mossy log along the edge of the forest. The survivor gratefully accepted a drink from Haley's copper canteen. "What can you tell us of this massacre?"

"The devils fell upon us in the middle of the night following the last Sabbath. The sentries never barked a cry of warning, their throats no doubt slit before they could raise a voice."

"Remain still," Greenheath said grasping the man's wounded shoulder. From his medicine bag he gathered a mix of bruised alder, crushed scarlet buckeye nuts and other ingredients to produce a poultice. Though he realized no care could ward off imminent death, he hoped that treating the injury might afford the victim some relief from pain in his final moments. "Those who attacked you," Greenheath said, "Can you describe them? Were they Cherokee warriors?"

"There were Cherokee in their ranks," the man said. He winced as Greenheath applied the poultice. "But this was no common war party. I recognized amongst them mainly renegades and fugitives. This small army consisted of runaway slaves, exiled Cherokee and Creek warriors, and assorted British and French deserters running from the conflict in the north." Tears streamed from the survivor's eyes as he recounted the carnage he had witnessed. "They slaughtered everyone, chased children into the forest, and hunted them like game animals. Even dawn could not curtail the bloodshed. When they finally sheathed their weapons, they collected a handful of carefully chosen maidens, bound and gagged them, and made for the mountains to the north with their spoils. Those are the ones I pity most, those five young women destined to suffer acts of perversion and debauchery in the savages' camp until death liberates them."

"Not if we can find them first," Haley promised, already scanning the surrounding woods for signs of recent passage. For the first time, he recognized from the man's torn vesture he had served as an itinerant preacher, traveling the borderlands delivering sermons and seeking converts. Though Haley rejected organized religion, he respected those who chose to lead a missionary life, admiring their faith and their fearlessness. "I'll swear to secure their emancipation or suffer death in doing so."

"If you possess the courage, then, cross the Odawadeesga Branch at Wayah Ford." Blood trickled out of the corner of the man's mouth. He shuddered with spasms as he coughed, fluids filling his chest. "Pick up their trail there—they do not need to cover their tracks. Their callousness and contemptible cruelty make the likelihood of pursuit almost unthinkable."

"We will find them and hold them accountable for this bloodbath." Greenheath gazed at his longtime friend, estimating the degree of his determination. For any two common men, no matter the profundity of their valor and frontier experience, such a vow would have amounted to no more than a fool's errand against insurmountable odds. Haley, though, showed no trace of fear. Greenheath reflected on his resolve as he nodded, expressing concurrence with Haley's oath. "Justice will be done."

"May God watch over you," the preacher said, a stillness settling over him as death neared. His eyelids fluttered and closed. "I came to this land as an evangelist, to bring the gospel to those whose circumstances had left them living in darkness for so long. After a lifetime of work, I die seeing that the shadows here are too rampant to scatter with benign sermons and urbane goodwill."

"Rest, now," Greenheath said. "Your work here is done."

Two: The Spanish Blockhouse

"For the few who survived the foredoomed expedition of 1509-1510, the preoccupation with exploration, adventure, and the beguiling search for wealth in the New World forever lost its allure. No promise of fame or gold could transcend the terrible memories of gore, grief, and turmoil suffered at the hands of bestial and degenerate primitives. The stigma of that discomfiture devastated the reputation of conquistador Diego Hernández de Salzedo and arrested further penetration into the region for half a century."

La odisea de Diego Hernández, Francisco Velázquez de Andagoya, 1675

Elijah Greenheath watched as twilight yielded to the approaching day. The subtle glow of morning's first light spread across the eastern horizon, staining the receding dusk and snuffing out the sparkling stars one by one.

Surrounded by pines, mountain laurel, and oaks, he and William Haley camped along the crest of a ridge that extended northeastward from the valley where they had discovered the ransacked settlement two days earlier. The intricate network of serpentine roots securing the trees to the windswept cliffs made for uncomfortable bedding, but the benefit of opting for defensible ground eclipsed all shortcomings. As company on the brief respite, ferns sprouted from unlikely fractures in the stone and lichen stretched across the gray faces of scattered boulders.

Greenheath had skirted the edges of the highlands in the past, traveled along both established trading routes and lesser-used game trails, and spent months in the wilderness living off the land where he regularly divested himself of all the fixtures and fittings of civilization. Still, he had never roamed so far into these mountains. Most settlers still shunned the region, where parallel ranges stretched for countless miles, punctuated by long, deep troughs carved by churning rivers. Even the Cherokee balked at building permanent villages beyond the Odawadeesga, their fears rooted in legends and myths passed from generation to generation and rarely shared with outsiders.

Greenheath knew the stories all too well, and had learned to pay them the respect they deserved. Each primitive legend, no matter how far-fetched, sprang from some long-forgotten seed of truth.

"There are places on this earth not meant for man." Greenheath offered his companion a hand. Morning mist met in darkened hollows beneath the mountains reluctant to yield to the dawn. Likewise, umbrageous sanctuaries the world over excluded illumination, clinging to primeval gloom to shield the last surviving vestiges of a protohistoric race. "These abominations of nature — the things which built citadels and cities long before the earliest nations of man matured — their intransience threatens our own fruition."

"The Great Old Ones endure, lingering in Stygian gloom, content to manipulate the flora and fauna of the waking world as it suits them." Haley had encountered such beings in his long years of service to Sodalitas Invictus, fought against them and their pathetic worshippers. "Though their sway is formidable, resistance is not wasted."

"I know," Greenheath said, still waiting for his first opportunity to face such a creature. "Ultimately, though, can our defiance keep them from reawakening?" The longstanding war remained deadlocked with neither party able to claim the smallest victory. Sodalitas Invictus, unwavering in its vow to rid the world of this blight, barely managed to contain the influence of the latent godlings. "Perhaps it is best not to ponder such abstract matters when we have a specific undertaking before us."

"Do you think we will find them in time?" Haley inspected his smoothbore musket, an old and trusted companion. He scratched his scalp before repositioning his black tricorne. Less inclined to eschew his aristocratic pedigree, his manner of dress distinguished him from Greenheath. He wore buckskin narrow-fall knee breeches, knit hose, and soft leather buskins. Having slept in the final hours before morning, he gathered his tailored coat, belt, cartridge box, and axe before slaking his thirst with water from his canteen. "It is possible that they have already been sacrificed."

"From the information enclosed in the dossier from the Duke of Newcastle-upon-Tyne, we must presuppose the alleged cultists we seek are unlikely to inflict injury upon their captives before the prescribed date of the ritual." Though Greenheath had spared the dying preacher details of their present assignment, the incident at Rowan had shed all his previous doubts about the legitimacy of recurring reports of slayings in outlying settlements and among villages of the region's indigenous people. At the start, he deemed the testimony no more than exaggerated accounts of conventional frontier raids and skirmishes, regrettable but routine occurrences. Even when the sporadic tales began to echo elements of Cherokee legends, Greenheath discounted the similarities. Over several months, the abundance and the indecency of the stories made them increasingly difficult to dismiss. Somewhere in the uncharted back country, an apocryphal group of zealots had reemerged from longstanding dormancy. "The misplaced fanaticism that drives this cluster of miscreants should make them adhere to the principles of the ceremony they intend to perform. As long as we can locate their lair before the autumnal equinox, we should find all their captives unharmed."

"That leaves us little time," Haley said. "The season will change in only two days' time."

"Let us trust that their method of reckoning time is as accurate as our own."

Upon receiving cryptic instructions from his secretive benefactors in England, Greenheath found himself obliged to further investigate the matter — to "handle the situation with equal parts discretion and determination." As a private abettor acting on behalf of the clandestine London-based cabal, Greenheath now understood this assignment could only end in violence. The profile the duke had provided left no prospect for either compromise or clemency.

Though the reputed history of the mountain-dwelling sect remained as ambiguous as it was implausible, the extermination of the group could not be deferred.

"Judging by their tracks, we are within a day's reach of them now," Haley said, eager to rejoin the hunt. Taking a few steps, he glanced over his shoulder. Greenheath stood, frozen in contemplation, stoic as the soaring spruce beneath which he reflected. "Is something vexing you?"

"We are perhaps hours away from a confrontation that will certainly end in chaos and indiscriminate killing." Greenheath patted his Kaintuck rifle, acknowledging its willingness to serve. He treated his weapon with reverence and fidelity. He preferred its accuracy to the outmoded imprecision of his partner's Brown Bess. Its sleek custom design—from its long octagonal barrel and small bore, to its stock made from tiger maple—lent it a quality of audaciousness. "Though the motivation is clear and the intended outcome is amenable, the righteousness of the act makes it no more palatable to me."

"We have worked together for many years, Elijah. Once, you considered me a mentor. In truth, I have gleaned as much knowledge from you as I have imparted to you." Haley regarded his former apprentice with the pride of a satisfied taskmaster. Realizing his son's potential significance, Greenheath's father had paired the two intentionally. Haley's guidance helped enhance Greenheath's intellectual propensity and reinforced his extraordinary perceptive skills. "We two are different from the common man. We are privy to things few could imagine. We are aware of confidential details of state that could incite revolution and topple governments. We are apprised of all the undisclosed facets of history that cause kings and queens to suffer sleepless nights." The secret society to which both men had sworn their allegiance harkened back to an epoch when civilization dissociated itself from the pursuit of knowledge, when wisdom which might have been forever lost had to be cached and concealed. "Even with the dawning of this age of enlightenment, the burden of confronting these dark legacies may always fall upon our shoulders—and upon the shoulders of those who follow in our footsteps."

"I sometimes wonder if this birthmark was more a curse than a blessing." Greenheath pulled back the self-fringed sleeve of his buckskin wamus to reveal a curious star-shaped blemish. At its center, an eye appeared to contain a tiny flame. His father had understood its meaning, recognized and explained its assurance of extraordinary mental capacity, amplified insightfulness, imposing physical strength and dexterity, and unconventional longevity. Along with the boon, though, came custodianship. "Despite all the inborn traits this mark guarantees, I regret that I was denied the choice of living a more ordinary existence."

"Even a Sentinel has the right of choice, Elijah." A hundred years earlier, Haley had struggled with his destiny, too. "I elected to serve the brotherhood, to do what had to be done to allow civilization to flourish." The elder Sentinel empathized with his younger partner's trepidation. Never before had Greenheath faced such a treacherous task. Never before had he met a foe so tainted by the darkest elements of the cosmos. "I know that compared to our past endeavors, this assignment must seem particularly disconcerting—and I will not deny that what lies ahead will surpass your innermost fears. You would be a fool not be concerned—but your resolve is not diminished because of it. You have already made your choice, years ago. The characteristics that lend us strength may be inherited, but our will is all our own."

Shrugging off his momentary disinclination, Greenheath returned to the task at hand.

****

Shortly before sunset, the men discerned a slender ribbon of smoke climbing into the evening sky amidst the laurel slicks of a broad valley. Standing on a blue-gray, slate-like promontory surrounded by a clump of blooming monk's hood, they beheld a deep gorge that stretched far toward a distant ridgeline, a sizable basin already half-bathed in the shadows of dusk. At the center of lowland, a peculiar granite dome swelled from the gently rolling forested floor.

With daylight quickly abating, the men began a wary but swift descent, passing along a dry wash choked with boulders and through a rhododendron tunnel. On the steep slope, Greenheath and Haley roved through stands of sand myrtle clutching the bare rock, continuously aware that though civilized men had seldom trod this remote hollow, the odds of encountering hostile entities increased with each passing moment.

Tracking the source of the smoke, Greenheath soon stumbled upon the smoldering remnants of what must have been a copious bonfire blazing through the previous night. At the center of the fire pit, the men identified three charred skulls. Surrounding the scene, scattered amidst a low understory of purple-berried pokeweeds, a macabre collection of bones on rancid entrails confirmed the disgraceful degeneracy of wanton cannibalism.

"This inhumanity leaves little doubt that those we pursue were accurately identified and described." Haley recalled with angst the portrayal of their quarry as detailed in the dossier channeled through Sodalitas Invictus. Its tradition, the Duke of Newcastle-upon-Tyne claimed, went back thousands of years to a time before recorded history. Its disciples originally consisted strictly of various indigenous peoples—expatriated natives coerced into ceremonial worship. More recently, the brotherhood believed their ranks had been augmented by discontented Europeans and various pariahs. "It is one matter for isolated indigenes to exhibit what must be deemed barbaric attributes. What I cannot fathom is how cultured men born of civilization can adopt and embrace such brutishness."

"Neither refinement nor edification confirms a capacity for morality or magnanimity," Greenheath said. Leaving his companion to pick through the bones of the cult's most recent victims, Greenheath discovered the silhouette of an unexpected edifice skulking in the darkness. There, amidst a tangle of briars and dog-hobble, an old, dilapidated Spanish blockhouse squatted on a small plateau overlooking the valley floor. "Follow me," he whispered, beckoning Haley. "I may have found their lair."

Both men sensed straining eyes mindful of their cautious approach, eyes anxiously watching them from an embrasure in the blockhouse. The quadrangular fortification had been ravaged by the callous elements of slowly passing years, subjected to the varying extremes of an ever-changing climate and the stubborn and steady repossession by the omnipresent wilderness.

The building's primitive construct offered further evidence of its considerable age. The vine-covered walls of the wooden palisades, interrupted by sporadic loopholes for musketry, showed signs of both an immemorial and a more recent siege. From his studies, Greenheath immediately recognized it as a vestige from one of two noted Spanish excursions in the area, both predating the English colony at Roanoke Island by many years—both episodes only marginally recorded by history and destined to be ultimately forgotten. Each adventure had ended in tragedy: Captain Juan Pardo lost all his troops to a native uprising in 1568; earlier, conquistador Diego Hernández de Salzedo's expedition set out to survey the mountains and abruptly vanished. Intermittent accounts gleaned from purported survivors of the 1510 campaign bore striking similarities to the many Cherokee legends which now seemed increasingly credible.

"A rather slapdash attempt at constructing a frontier garrison — its original occupants must have found their way to the grave long ago." Signaling Greenheath to take a defensive position, Haley crouched behind a black cherry tree. Continuing in a whisper, he added "It is not large enough to house the numbers I would expect to find participating in the clan we seek. The rogues may use the blockhouse as a sentry point, though, to warn the others of an incursion."

"Do we attack?"

"No — we wait. The sound of battle would only serve to draw in additional combatants." Though Haley remained confident that their combined ingenuity and agility would prevail against an enemy benefited by large numbers, he saw no logic in hastening the looming mêlée. A deft strategist, he planned to stalk the eremitic cultists from the shadows, eliminating as many as possible before conducting a decisive raid on their retreat. "If they know we are in their territory, they will come to us."

Silence lingered as stars began to fill the heavens, aligning themselves in predetermined patterns forming familiar constellations. Rifle in hand, Greenheath pressed his back against the mossy trunk of a birch, his attention briefly beguiled by the mesmerizing display of stellar grandeur. Beyond the thin canopy of the forest, beyond the sparse wispy clouds and the invariable orbit of earth's subordinate moon, the boundless universe sprawled endlessly, content knowing that even in the expanse of eternity only a fraction of its mysteries could be unlocked.

Greenheath knew that science might ultimately take future generations to the far-flung stars. Having studied legends asserting the existence of extraterrestrial spawn locked in earthly exile — bound, caged, imprisoned, or withdrawn — he knew, too, such explorers along that grim perimeter would face countless horrors in a noble but fundamentally futile effort to conquer the unknown.

Little time had elapsed when the soft sound of inconsolable sorrow drifted from the blockhouse. Staggered weeping and muffled voices gradually filled the darkened stockade, echoing amidst the rafters.

"Friend or foe?"

The query reverberated only a short distance in the thick, rugged woods.

"Friend," Haley responded, recognizing both the accent and the undeniable mark of civility in the man's hail. Instinct afforded him the luxury of provisional trust, and he lowered his musket.

"Approach — but be quick about it."

Inside, Greenheath and Haley found the vestiges of a British expeditionary force apparently sent into the mountains to suppress the warring Cherokee. A contingent of 124 men under the command of Colonel Benjamin Waddel had stumbled upon the valley even as the cold-blooded cultists returned from their recent raid on Rowan.

"Not men — they were like animals." A rank-and-file soldier, identifying himself as Erastus Peters, described the ensuing skirmish. "They had at their disposal every manner of firearm, yet they favored crude hatchets and spears and rocks. They came at us with such fury that we had time for but one fusillade. Our bullets rained down on them like leaden hail, but they attacked nonetheless."

"This is all that remain?" Greenheath looked into the faces of the four men cowering in the blockhouse. Fear had kept them from full retreat, shackled them into the false security offered by the old fortification.

"There were seven of us—last night, they claimed the other three." The soldier trembled as he spoke. His companions shrank in silence, too frightened to interject any personal observations. "One moment they were here, among us—the next, they were gone. We don't know how the monsters carried them off without disturbing us." Peters cringed as he recalled the long night. "We heard their unbearable screams resonate through the darkness, heard their pleas for either deliverance or prompt death. Upon hearing such excruciating torment, no man could hope to summon courage. We dared not leave this shelter lest we share their fate."

"How many attacked you?"

"Dozens—Cherokee and Creek and Choctaw fighting right alongside French and British and Spanish." He paused, rubbed his eyes as if trying to expel a particular image from his mind. "Some of them were different, though, I swear it. Some were beasts or devils. The man who claimed to be their leader called them his Uquedaligeesdee, his Servitors of Chaos."

"Who commands them?" Greenheath recognized the Cherokee word from recitations of old legends. In his studies of medieval grimoires, he had also come across repeated references to the cryptic Servitors of Chaos. Spread throughout the pages of assorted rare occult treatises in diverse citations, these pagans were categorized as worshipers of a single, subterranean deity and were notorious for their enactment of a particularly hideous communal ceremony. Originally concentrated within some antediluvian society lost to history, they dispersed into smaller tribes during one of the violent cataclysms dividing the great ages of man. In nomadic clans, they spread to the farthest reaches of the world where they went into hibernation. "Who called them by that name?"

"Their leader—a dark-skinned man who speaks fluent English. He calls himself Zhaig." Peters paused, turned toward a nearby loophole. Reluctantly, he peered out the breach and scanned the murky darkness rife with nebulous shadow. "He will be here soon enough. He will come to taunt as he did last night. He will come to claim us, to loose his savages on us. By God, we will all beg for the succor of expeditious death before this night is finished."

As if invoked by Peters' confession of fear, the bloodcurdling howls of prowling cultists, actively stalking the wild darkness outside the blockhouse, shattered the relative silence leaving no one unaware of the forthcoming struggle for survival.

To be continued...

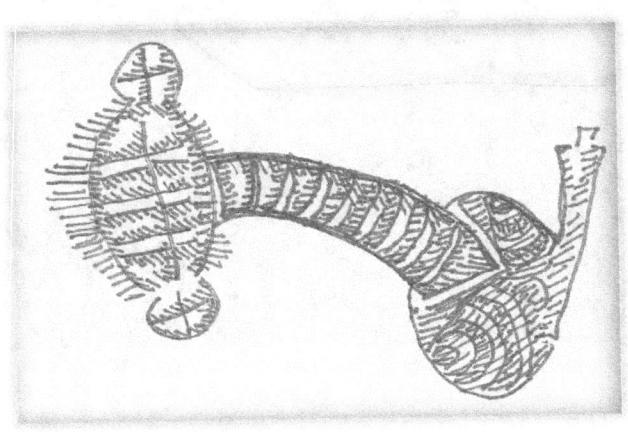

My Master Calls by Marge Simon

His voice through the blue twilight,
I sense him with every heartbeat.
Once, I made a small mistake,
And he was disapproving.
Tonight, I get to make it up.

I've brought Robert for the Change,
Having passed my tests so well,
An apt student, surely willing,
Being so in love with me
To relinquish his mortality.

My master smiles with satisfaction,
For Bob's a healthy specimen, not too bright.
Proudly he submits,
Becomes another Renfield.
Now whatever Master's needs,
He shall provide.

Santa Claus and Snowflake
by
Christopher T. Dabrowski

Santa Claus wondered if Snowflake was truly attracted to him or whether she was fond of him because he always had some gifts for her.

He found their relationship a bit suspicious—he was old, grey-haired, and had a big belly. Yet some prefer older men, so....

Whatever the case, he decided to get in shape and groom himself anyway. He bought a pass and went to the gym. *Holidays are coming, so I need to get in shape to have the strength to cram gifts,* he decided. He picked up a barbell and felt a sudden strong pressure in his chest...

The End

IT CAME FROM INSIDE THE INKWELL! By Vincent Davis

"SINCE IT'S YOUR FIRST DAY ON THE JOB, HERE'S SOME HELPFUL ADVICE, KEEP YOUR EXPECTATIONS LOW."

Small Differences
by
Christopher T. Dabrowski

She'd be beautiful except for those tendrils and a segmented shell on her back.

"You said you loved me and accepted our differences..."

"Yes, but..." Well, how can I persuade her to remove these accessories? Yes, I love her, but these differences inhibit my lust. All because of the damn aliens!

Intelligent insects are residing on the neighbouring planet. UFOs have been there. Now it's clear what this was for—a hybrid species, half-human and half-insect, created and placed on a terra-formed planet.

While I understand scientific experimentation, they went solidly overboard with this one.

The End

About the Contributors

Linda Barrett:

Ms. Barrett has been writing all her life. She wrote her first book at the age of eight. It's still in the McKinley Elementary school library. She was published in the *Huntingdon Junior Library* literary magazine by age thirteen. She's won three awards with the Montgomery County Community College Writer's contest. "Mr. Cat's Revenge" won third place in the 2014 MCCC contest. Ms. Barrett lives with her 84 years young mother in Abington in the same house for 50 years."

Rajeev Bhargava:

Rajeev Bhargava has been writing since birth and is now a creative multi-genre writer and artist. His career includes public articles, illustrations, poems, and stories published in dark fantasy and horror, science fiction and fantasy, an assorted poems and haiku collection of love and romance, comedy, wit, and humor and the welfare of animals, plants and concern for our green environment. Just recently, he completed a children's storybook for Christmas, Easter, and Halloween, all under the pen name Silver Phoenix. Rajeev's first work, a dark fantasy chiller, appeared in 1990 for *Peeping Tom* titled "Old Crow." Rajeev is thankful to Jesus for his talent; he's working on a new book this Halloween titled *Terrifying and Bloodcurdling Scary Stories for Sshh!!! …It's Halloween*. Rajeev is single and lives with his parents and five pet Chihuahuas. He's writing a romantic novel entitled *Love Will Find a Way*. He's attained an Arts and Humanities BA (HONS) in Literature and an English Literature Teaching Certificate. When he's not writing, he enjoys video, photography, acting, fashion, modeling, ceramics, and pottery.

Margaret L. Carter:

Reading *Dracula* at the age of twelve ignited Margaret L. Carter's interest in a wide range of speculative fiction and inspired her to become a writer. Vampires, however, have always remained close to her heart. Her work on vampirism in literature includes four books and numerous articles. She holds a PhD in English from the University of California (Irvine), and her dissertation contained a chapter on *Dracula*. In fiction, she has written horror, fantasy, and paranormal romance, as well as sword-and-sorcery fantasy in collaboration with her husband, a retired naval officer. Recent publications include *Against the Dark Devourer* (Lovecraftian dark paranormal romance), spring-themed contemporary light fantasy *Bunny Hunt*, Victorian Christmas romance *A Ghost in the Green Bestiary*, and light paranormal romance *Summertide Echoes*. Her short stories have appeared in various anthologies, including the "Darkover" and "Sword and Sorceress" series. She and her husband live in Maryland and have four children, several grandchildren and great-grandchildren, and two cats. Please visit Carter's Crypt: http://www.margaretlcarter.com

Christopher T. Dabrowski:

Christopher has had numerous books published in the USA and Poland. His USA works include: *Anomaly* and *Escape*, both published by the Royal Hawaiian Press. Books published in Poland include *Anima Vilis* (Initium), *Grobbing* (Novae Res), *Deathbirth and other Stories* (Agharta & Amoryka), *Orgazmokalipsa* (Alternatywne publishing house), *Anomalia* (Forma publishing house), and *Ucieczka* (2017 - Dom Horroru publishing house). Monika Olasek provided the English translation for his *Night to Dawn* stories.

Sandy DeLuca:

Sandy has written five novels; *Settling in Nazareth* (she painted the cover art), *Descent, Manhattan Grimoire, From Ashes,* and *Requiem for the Dead*. Her poetry chapbook, *Burial Plot in Sagittarius* (also created cover art and illustrations), was nominated for the BRAM STOKER award in 2001. Her art has been exhibited in galleries, hair salons, book stores and online venues. She has also painted covers and contributed interior illustrations for various numerous small press venues.

Kendall Evans:

Kendall Evans' stories and poems have appeared in nearly all the major science fiction and fantasy magazines, including *Asimov's SF, Analog, Weird Tales, Strange Horizons, Weirdbook, Mythic Delirium, Dreams & Nightmares, Space & Time, Nebula Award Showcase (2012), The Magazine of Speculative Poetry, Amazine Stories, Fantastic Stories, Spectral Realms* and many others. He is the author of the novels *The Rings of Ganymede* and *The Adventures of Ching Shih, Pirate Princess.*

Chris Friend:

Chris has published his art in small press horror magazines for nearly 25 years. His surreal horror images have been featured in *Stygian Articles, Realm of the Vampire, Deathrealm, Black Petals,* and *Space and Time.* He draws his inspiration from Harry Clarke, H. R. Giger, and the horror comics of the 70s such as the Tomb of Dracula her and the Hammer Studios Frankenstein films. Chris friend can be reached at Mars_art_13@yahoo.com. Chris friend can be reached at Mars_art_13@yahoo.com.

To sample his illustrations, go to http://chris.michaelherring.net and http://www.moonlit-path.com/art-2-13-06.htm.

Charles Gramlich:

Charles Gramlich writes from the piney woods of southern Louisiana and is the author of the Talera fantasy series, the post-apocalyptic SF novel *Razored Land,* and eight books under the penname A. W. Hart in the Concho Texas Ranger series. Many of his short stories have been collected in the anthologies, *Bitter Steel,* (fantasy), *Midnight in Rosary* (Vampires/Werewolves), and *In the Language of Scorpions* (Horror). Charles's work is generally available through Amazon, Barnes & Noble, and Wildside Press. He blogs at http://charlesgramlich.blogspot.com and is happy to connect on Facebook.

Todd Hanks:

The creative writing of Todd Hanks has been seen in publications such as Asimov's Science Fiction Magazine and the Kansas City Star newspaper.

Hal Kempka:

Hal's stories have been published in numerous magazines and ezines including *Night to Dawn, Blood Moon Rising, Black Petals, Inner Sins, Sanitarium, Yellow Mama,* and *Microhorror.* His horror short fiction anthologies, *Blue Plate Special* and *Discarded Treasures,* are currently available on Amazon Kindle, Barnes and Noble, and Smashwords, among others. *Discarded Treasures* is available in both paperback and e-book. Other anthologies including his stories are Pill Hill Press: *Zombie Art Inspired Short Stories, Blood Bound Books: Seasons in the Abyss,* and Post Mortem Press: *Shadowplay.*

April Lafleur:

April Lafleur's distinctive painting style is inspired by German Expressionism, emphasizing the artist's deep-rooted feelings or ideas, evoking powerful reactions-abandoning reality, characterized by simplified shapes, bright colors, gestural marks and brush strokes. Masters like Kirshner and Marc come to mind when viewing April's dynamic paintings.

April has earned an AFA at the Community College of Rhode Island, where she had the privilege of studying with Bob Judge, a masterful painter who has worked as an artist for over sixty years. He continues to mentor and inspire her today. In addition, she studied art at Rhode Island College. Today, her paintings are maintained in private collections. She exhibits in New England presently and is working to place her figurative work with print magazines beyond the local area.

Her studio is located at the Agawam Mill in Rhode Island, where she works long hours to perfect her craft. Website: www.aprillafleurart.com.

Hillary Lyon:

With an MA in English Literature from SMU, Hillary Lyon founded and for 20 years served as senior editor for the independent poetry publisher, Subsynchronous Press. Her speculative, horror, and sci-fi stories have appeared in numerous print and online publications. She's also an illustrator for horror/sci-fi, and pulp fiction sites. And she loves to hand-paint furniture and accessories.

Rod Marsden:

Rod Marsden hails from Sydney, Australia. He has three degrees related to writing and history. His stories have been published in Australia, England, Russia, the USA and now Canada. He has work in the American anthology *Cats Do it Better*, the American steam punk anthology *Break Time* and in the Canadian anthology *Morbid Metamorphosis*. Many of his short stories have been published in *Night to Dawn* magazine. His books include *Undead Reb Down Under and Other Vampire Stories, Disco Evil: Dead Man's Stand, Ghost Dance*, and *Desk Job* (his salute to Lewis Carroll). *Cold Water Conscience* is his venture into Crime/Horror. His short play, *Zombie Vision*, was well received at Cronulla Arts Theatre. His play *Hyde and Seek* was even better received. Rod has a fondness for Cronulla and the Wollongong area but an abiding love for the more northern Clarence River region of his home state of New South Wales.

Denny E. Marshall:

Denny E. Marshall has had art, poetry, and fiction published. Some recently. Denny mostly draws.

Elizabeth Hattie Pierce-Collins:

Elizabeth first learned art and drawing from her mother. From there, she was self-taught until she was able to attend art school. She loves drawing the human figure and never stops studying the human body in motion. Her illustrations have appeared in *Night to Dawn* magazine and *The Spider's Web* (a novel). These have drawn positive attention from the readers. Elizabeth hopes to appear in more magazines and books in the future. For more information, contact Elizabeth at wackyursalinan45@aol.com.

Marc Shapiro:

Marc Shapiro is within spitting distance of 100 published books. Recent additions include the books *Bukowski: On Film, Pete Brown: The Poet Who Rocks*, and coming next year, *Abracadabra: The Steve Miller Story*. Also lurking in the shadows: *Atomic Rooster*. When Marc Shapiro works, he works hard. By the time you read this, he will have written a hundred more.

Marge Simon:

Marge Simon's works appear in publications such as DailySF Magazine, Pedestal, Dreams& Nightmares. She edits a column for the HWA Newsletter, "Blood & Spades: Poets of the Dark Side," and serves as Chair of the Board of Trustees. She won the Strange Horizons Readers Choice Award, 2010, and the SFPA's Dwarf Stars Award, 2012. She has won three Bram Stoker Awards ® for Superior Work in Poetry, two first place Rhysling Awards and the Grand Master Award from the SF Poetry Association, 2015. In addition to her poetry, she has published two prose collections: *Christina's World*, Sam's Dot Publications, 2008 and *Like Birds in the Rain*, Sam's Dot, 2007. Her poems appear in *Qualia Nous* (Written Backwards), *The Dark Phantastique* (Jasunni Productions), Spectral Realms anthologies by S.T. Joshi, and more poems will appear in *Chiral Mad 3* and *Scary Out There*, a HWA/ Simon & Schuster Y/A collection, 2015. www.margesimon.com

Matthew Wilson:

Matthew Wilson has been published repeatedly in *Star*Line, Night to Dawn Magazine, Hiraeth Publishing*, and many more. His first story collection, *Gargoyles of the Abbey*, is now available on kindle.

Lee Clark Zumpe:

Lee Clark Zumpe has been writing and publishing horror, dark fantasy and speculative fiction since the late 1990s. His short stories and poetry have appeared in a variety of publications such as *Weird Tales, Space and Time* and *Dark Wisdom*; and in anthologies such as *Dark Horizons, Best New Zombie Tales Vol. 3, Dread Shadows in Paradise, Heroes of Red Hook* and *World War Cthulhu*. His work has earned several honorable mentions in *The Year's Best Fantasy and Horror* collections.

An entertainment columnist with Tampa Bay Newspapers, Lee has penned hundreds of film, theater and book reviews and has interviewed novelists as well as music industry icons such as Paddy Moloney of The Chieftains and Alan Parsons. His work for TBN has been recognized repeatedly by the Florida Press Association, including a first-place award for criticism in the 2013 Better Weekly Newspaper Contest. Lee lives on the west coast of Florida with his wife and daughter. Visit www.leeclarkzumpe.com.